The F

The Park Place Rangers A Series of Short Stories

Larry Watts

Larry Dean Watts Publishing

The Park Place Rangers
A Series of Short Stories

Copyright © May, 2013 by Larry Watts

First Edition: January 2014

All rights reserved. No part of this publication may be reproduced, stored in a retrieval system, or transmitted, in any form or by any means, electronic, mechanical, photocopy, recording, or otherwise, without written permission of the author.

Inquiries to
Larry Dean Watts Publishing
2874 Morning Pond Lane
Dickinson, TX 77539

ISBN -13 978-0-9890859-3-9

Library of Congress Control Number: 2013921422

This is a work of fiction. All characters depicted herein are fictional and the product of the author's imagination. All events portrayed are also fictional drawn from the author's many years working within the law enforcement community in Texas.

Published in the United States

Special thanks to my wife Carolyn; and to my friends and fellow authors Tom Rizzo, Gloria Hander Lyons, and René Palmer Armstrong, for assisting me with editing these stories and encouraging me to write.

Just as importantly, thanks to all the Houston police officers who served at the Park Place police substation sometime during their career. I especially appreciate those who reminded me of the tales of enjoyment, sadness, and life experiences that took place when the Park Place Rangers were on the prowl.

Larry Watts

TABLE OF CONTENTS

Larry Watts

RITES OF PASSAGE

At 10:45 p.m. Eddie Jackson walked in the back door of the Park Place police substation in Houston carrying his ditty bag and a short-barreled pump shotgun. He hadn't scored for a locker yet to keep his equipment in, so he was carrying it back and forth from home. His shift started in 15 minutes and he was ready to begin his second week as a Park Place Ranger.

A year and nine months into his career as a police officer, Eddie had managed to snag his dream assignment at Park Place. Not only did he live near the substation, making the commute to work a short 15 minutes, but he could now call himself a Park Place Ranger; the informal, but highly-regarded designation for those officers who worked the southeast side of Houston.

The nickname was probably a holdover from the name of the substation's softball team a few years earlier, but when the station began getting a reputation as a no-nonsense crime suppression unit, the tag Park Place Rangers took on new meaning. Several officers told Eddie different stories about how the nickname came to be and each of them was absolutely sure that his version was the truth. It made no difference to Eddie, however, because what it meant to him was to be identified with a group of officers who took their jobs seriously and didn't mind bending the rules to get it done, sort of a Clint Eastwood/Dirty Harry approach to law enforcement.

Eddie rounded the corner of the hallway leading into the large, open lobby that was energized by a gathering of blue-clad men reporting for night-shift duty or checking in at the end of their evening-shift tour. A desk officer, assigned to answer the phone and take walk-in reports from citizens, sat behind a long, bar-height counter.

Eddie's eyes were drawn to a figure moving stealthily toward evening-shift officer Grady Henson standing in front of the desk. Henson, sipping from the cup of coffee in his hand and talking with the desk officer, did not see the figure behind him. Jack Smith approached as a child might sneak up on a bird about to fly away. Comprehending the drill, Eddie immediately made a wide arc around the front desk just as Smith goosed Grady Henson, while simultaneously yelling, "Get 'em!"

Responding exactly as his co-workers had anticipated, Grady flung the coffee cup to his right, bellowing, "Son of a bi..!" The cup hit the cinder block wall, breaking and slinging coffee over a 10-foot area. Lucky for Eddie, he was out of the way before the cup flew through the air.

The group of about fifteen officers broke into raucous laughter at the antics of Jack Smith and at Henson's response; that is until the lieutenant's door swung open and Lieutenant C.V. Johnson stepped out. Johnson stared at the coffee drenched wall and floor, littered with scattered shards of broken glass glistening in the artificial light.

His scowling face reddened as he growled, "What's going on out here?"

"Oh, nothing really, boss. Grady just spilled his coffee again," offered Jack Smith as he walked toward the officers' locker room, avoiding the lieutenant's stare, but winking at the officers who could see his face.

The lieutenant turned his head to glare at each officer. As his mouth opened to make further comments, a man and woman walked in to report an automobile accident. Johnson retreated to his office and shut the door.

Eddie entered the roll-call room where officers gathered at the beginning of each shift to receive their assigned beat, a partner for the night, and designated patrol car (or 'shop' in cop language) they would be driving. Most of the officers were still laughing and engaging in small talk about the broken cup, spilled coffee and the look on the lieutenant's face when he opened his door.

Standing behind a small wooden podium, Sergeant Paul Dirksen attended to roll-call duties. The Sergeant, slightly overweight with a constant cynical expression on his face, began.

"Alright, enough B.S., let's get this over with. You all realize I have to spend the rest of the night here at the station with the lieutenant and he's not happy about all the shenanigans in the lobby. Someday one of you is going to get hurt with all the grab-ass pranks you pull out there."

The sergeant gave a short update on activity from the previous shift before making assignments. Eddie's brow furrowed with disappointment when he heard that he was assigned to ride in one of the slowest districts in the Park Place substation's coverage area. That was bad enough, but then he learned he would be riding with Jack Smith.

He had never partnered with Jack, but Eddie didn't care for the constant cutting-up and practical jokes. He believed their work was much too serious for clowning around. Jack was not known to volunteer for calls or try to find a little extra excitement on the streets when things were slow. Those facts, coupled with their assignment to a slow district on a Sunday night, caused Eddie to anticipate a boring shift.

As the two men loaded their equipment into the police car, Jack asked Eddie whether he wanted to drive or ride shotgun. On the night-shift, the norm, set by tradition, was that the driver answered the radio while the passenger wrote tickets and made reports. Eddie chose to drive.

"So, do you like working Park Place?" Jack asked.

"Yeah, I've wanted to be here since I was in the academy." Eddie responded. "I love working at Park Place, but I'd prefer working Sunnyside or the ship-channel district to being here in District 14. There won't be much going on tonight."

"Yeah, I know. The first three or four years you can't wait for that next call or to catch that next burglar or hi-jacker." Jack said. "But now that I've been here for 15 years I realize that I don't want to be a hero. I just want to go home to my kids each morning after work and to know I did my job. Working in a slower district makes it more likely that I'll get to do that than working busier districts. You young guys can be the hotdogs."

Eddie considered these few serious remarks he had ever heard Jack make. Apparently he didn't care for the 'Dirty Harry' approach to police work. So what? Eddie intended to make a difference during his career. Jack could call him a hotdog, but he wouldn't take the bait. He'd just try to make the shift without arguing with the older officer.

The radio was quiet except for a disturbance call to a bar at 75th Street and South Harbor, down by the ship channel. Eddie wished they were working that district so they could slide by and see what was happening. No calls, no traffic on the streets – a typical Sunday night. Most people were at home in order to be ready for work on Monday morning. Even those who went to the bars on Sunday night usually were home by 11 or so.

Little conversation had taken place since the initial exchange when they started the shift. At 1:30 in the morning, after patrolling through residential neighborhoods most of the shift, the monotony was finally broken when they received a call on the radio. The dispatcher advised them to report to Park Place substation to make the mail run, a nightly assignment often given to one of the units in a slower district. It involved transferring prisoners and paperwork to the central police station in downtown Houston. When they arrived at the substation they learned that there were no prisoners to transport so they would literally be the mail carrier for the next hour or so.

With only a handful of paperwork to be delivered to the central police station, Jack carried it out and threw it in the seat between himself and Eddie. Eddie shifted the car into drive and made a right turn out of the station. He drove about a block to the intersection of Park Place Boulevard and Reveille Street where he stopped the patrol car in the left turn lane to wait for a green light.

The vehicle barely came to a stop when the dispatcher broke the silence with a call that always got officers' attention.

"All units, a robbery in progress at the U-Totem store in the 7100 block of Park Place. 732 make the call."

Eddie checked traffic and gunned the engine, maneuvering the car out of the left turn lane and continuing straight on Park Place Boulevard as he advised the dispatcher that they would back up the other car. They were only two blocks away.

Jack reached for his shotgun, wedged between their car seats. "Circle and come up on Poplar Street." he ordered. "Let me out on the corner before you pull in the parking lot."

Eddie, surprised at his partner's sudden burst of energy, followed the instructions, enabling Jack to jump from the car as it slowed at the corner. After giving his partner a few seconds to get to the store, Eddie turned onto Park Place and pulled into the lot. As he did, he saw Jack jogging from the side of the building, heading for the front door. There appeared to be no one inside.

Jack opened the door and walked in as Eddie exited the patrol car with his shotgun in hand. As Jack entered the store, a tall white male with a pock-marked face, stepped from behind a display of soft drinks stacked to the right of the entrance.

Eddie, who was now nearly to the front door, saw Jack raise his shotgun, but the man aimed and fired a pistol into his face while the shotgun was still in motion. Jack collapsed like a rag doll.

Eddie came through the door shooting. He had five shells loaded in the shotgun. The first shell was a deer slug; the second, "double-aught" buckshot; and each shell after that alternated between the two. With the adrenalin controlling his actions, he didn't stop shooting until he had pumped the shotgun twice and heard the firing pin click because the weapon was empty. The suspect lay sprawled on the floor, half his lower face blown away and his chest torn to shreds by the buckshot.

Eddie threw the shotgun down and knelt over Jack. Unlike the suspect's body, Jack had only a single small dark red spot neatly centered between his eyes about ½ of an inch above the brow. He knew Jack was dead, but used his hand-held radio to call the dispatcher.

"Officer Down! Get me an ambulance out here." he shouted into the radio.

Within seconds dozens of police cars and wreckers arrived on the scene with emergency lights and spotlights glaring, making the parking lot a tiny spot of daylight surrounded by the blackest of nights. Two minutes later an ambulance operated by Houston firefighters arrived. They worked over Jack for a few minutes before one of them looked at Eddie and shook his head.

“Transport him!” Eddie screamed. “He’s not lying on this floor with that piece of shit while they work the crime scene!”

Eddie’s outburst was so forceful, the two firefighters immediately loaded Jack’s body onto the gurney that a second ambulance unit had wheeled into the store. Within seconds the sound of the siren filled the air as the ambulance sped off to Hermann Hospital. The firefighters, like police officers, understood that sometimes the rules just got in the way.

The rest of the night and most of the next day were a blur to Eddie; he moved through it as if he were a zombie. Eddie and the night manager of the convenience store, who had been slapped across the face with a pistol by the hi-jacker before Jack and Eddie arrived, made statements to Homicide investigators.

Three days later Eddie Jackson attended Jack Smith’s funeral with several hundred other Houston officers. A contingent from other cities as far away as Kansas City, Kansas, journeyed to Houston to honor a fallen brother. Eddie had an opportunity to speak with Jack’s widow and each of his three children. He knew that nothing he could say would help them on this day, but he repeated the same thing to each of the children.

"You should always remember that your father was a reluctant hero. All he really wanted to do was come home every morning to see you. Police officers aren't paid for what they do. They are paid for what they are willing to do if called on. Your Dad answered the call when it came."

As is always the case when a police officer or firefighter is killed in the line of duty, Jack Smith's funeral was an event to behold. News cameras filmed the several miles long funeral procession from the church the Smith family attended. Every City Council member and most city department heads were in attendance. The widow flinched at each burst from the rifles fired by the Honor Guard in salute to the fallen officer. The flag that was draped over the coffin was folded and presented to her. Kind words were privately spoken to Mrs. Smith and the children by the police chief.

When that day ended, however, life went on for all the attendees as it had before the shooting except for the widow, her children and Eddie Jackson. They were left to heal over the next months and years, having experienced the most brutal of events when a young husband, father and police partner was taken so swiftly from them.

Eddie was debriefed by a police psychologist the following week. When asked how he felt about having taken a life, he responded, "I don't even think about it. What I think about is Jack. I couldn't get there quick enough to save him. All the rest of what went on is just noise. No regrets for what I did. Just questions about what else I could have done.

"You know, I didn't want to ride with him that night, because I didn't think he was aggressive enough. He just knew something about being aggressive that I didn't understand. He wanted to catch that hi-jacker and was just as excited as I was to make the call."

A month after the funeral his shift was walking out of the roll-call room preparing to begin another night on the streets of Houston; Sergeant Dirksen stopped Eddie and asked him to step into his office. When they were both seated, Dirksen began.

"Eddie, I want you to know that you did everything you could. Sometimes the only thing left to do for your partner is to take out the bad guy. At Park Place it counts when you do what you have to do. That's why we call ourselves the Rangers!"

Larry Watts

SNAKE WOMAN

Wayne Hartman began his patrol shift at 10 o'clock on Monday evening. Another slow night for police work in Houston; in another 30 minutes even the sparse traffic still on the street would be gone now that the bars had closed. He had written two tickets before midnight, that being the magic number needed to keep the sergeant off his butt about not getting enough arrests.

An aggressive cop who worked hard when there was action on the street, Wayne was not a good example for how Park Place Rangers conducted their business. If things were slow he was more likely to play than to patrol the streets. His personal life was a mess with two divorces and now in a third marriage that was about to come apart. Both of his most recent marriages had been to women he'd met working the midnight shift. The first was a waitress at a bar on his beat, and his current wife, an emergency room nurse at the hospital just a few blocks from the substation.

His supervisors rarely assigned a rookie to ride with him for fear of instilling his bad habits in new recruits. Many veteran officers preferred not to ride with him, but there was a muted respect.

Early in his career Wayne had saved his partner's life after both were shot when they were dispatched to a family disturbance call. They had been confronted on the front porch by a man with a shotgun who fired twice as he rushed out the door toward them. Wayne had been hit in the shoulder; the wound that still bothered him years later. His partner lost an eye and was struck in the neck by a pellet that nicked the left carotid artery. After shooting and killing the suspect, Wayne's actions to slow the loss of blood from his partner's neck wound were credited by doctors as saving his life.

Wayne pulled off Telephone Road into the parking lot of the Four Palms Club and began slowly driving through the huge lot to the exit at the other end. Known by officers who worked the area as a bar where women went to get picked up, he wondered if there might be one who had struck out and was leaving alone tonight. But this wasn't his lucky night. The parking lot was virtually empty already; the only people he saw were a man and woman about to enjoy their first, and maybe only, night with each other. He stopped his patrol car for a moment to see if they would forego a hotel room and do it right there on the trunk of the car they leaned against. In a moment, though, they disentangled, got into the car, and drove away.

He pulled out of the parking lot and drove slowly south on Telephone Road. As he approached the Roseland Club, a strip joint that had just closed, the headlights of a parked car turned on. As the car pulled onto Telephone Road in front of him, he noticed that the driver was a female. One taillight was not working, so Wayne turned on his overhead emergency lights and pulled close to the rear of the car. The driver pulled to the side of the road.

Wayne exited his car and walked to just behind the driver's door.

"See your license and insurance card?" he asked.

"Sure babe. What'd I do?" the rather attractive thirtyish redhead responded, reaching for her purse. "I don't think I was speeding, because I just left work right back there," she said as she handed him the documents and smiled.

Wayne glanced at both, seeing that they were valid and noting the driver's name, he said, "You got a tail light burned out and need to get it fixed. So, are you a stripper at the Roseland, Jackie?"

As she took the documents back, she responded, "Well, I don't consider myself a stripper. I'm a dancer and a contortionist and I use my boa constrictor in my act.

"Most of the girls now days just get on the stage with pasties and a G-string and hump a pole. But I'm a performer; still come out with a gown and evening gloves to let my audience enjoy watching me undress before twisting my body into a pretzel and letting Studley intertwine his body with mine."

Seeing a questioning look on Wayne's face, she added, "Studley's my snake. He's right here in this basket." She patted a tall woven basket that was setting in the seat beside her.

"No way! You don't let a snake crawl all over you!" Wayne was enjoying the conversation.

"Sure do. You should come by the Club sometime to watch my act. You might learn something." Jackie said with a mischievous grin.

"Well, I got a better idea. Why don't you give the police a little private performance?"

Wayne gave her that cocky smile that he so often found would work to ease into a more personal conversation with a new female acquaintance.

"You mean now?" Jackie asked. "Just where do you think we could do that? I don't think you want to see my performance right here in the middle of Telephone Road."

The conversation became a game of cat and mouse, with both Wayne and Jackie trying to play the part of the cat.

"Follow me over to where they're constructing the new loop. We'll go around the barricades and onto the overpass. It's nearly finished and we won't be disturbed up there. I'll call a couple of other guys over; they'll enjoy seeing you and the big snake."

Wayne turned and walked to his car before Jackie could answer. He knew she would follow.

As he drove toward their destination, Wayne called two other Park Place cars on the radio and told them to take the back channel. Officers used this channel for more private conversation because it was rarely monitored by the dispatcher or supervisors. When both units acknowledged that they had switched channels, Wayne said,

"Meet me on top of Long Drive. I've got some entertainment."

The drivers of both patrol units advised that they would meet him. Everyone on the night-shift knew that *'on top of Long Drive'* was code for the construction area where the new 610 Loop was being built. Once on top of the overpass the vehicles couldn't be seen by motorists below. Since the construction wasn't complete, they would skirt the barricades and drive up the newly constructed off-ramp that would one day be used by motorists to exit the Loop onto Long Drive.

Wayne glanced in his rear view mirror to be sure Jackie's car was still following. They wove their way to the new concrete slab that would eventually serve as the overpass. Both the other patrol cars were just behind them.

Billy Williamson and Eddie Jackson parked and got out first. Billy was the senior partner and had not consulted Eddie before agreeing to meet Wayne.

As they were driving to the meeting, Eddie thought about Jack Smith, a cop who had been killed one night while he and Eddie were riding together. Eddie never forgot that he had not wanted to ride with Jack that night. He thought Jack was too much of a jokester and didn't take police work serious enough. Eddie wasn't crazy about meeting with Wayne Hartman for whatever shenanigans he was engineering, but he wouldn't voice his displeasure. He still carried guilt about not wanting to ride with Jack. Regardless of whether he approved of his practical jokes, when the time came, Jack had been a real cop. Eddie had learned to reserve his criticism of others as a result.

Tom Bradley and his rookie, Pete Tarleton, exited their car and the four officers watched Wayne approaching with Jackie Sinclair in tow. She was carrying the woven basket that contained Studley. Wayne took the basket and set it on the trunk of Billy and Eddie's patrol car.

"Hey, guys. Meet Jackie Sinclair. She's going to put on a performance for us and we need a stage. Rookie, get that piece of plywood over there and put it on top of these four barrels," Wayne said as he pointed to a sheet of plywood that had been used as a form for pouring concrete.

Wayne never considered whether the other officers would want to be a part of his theatrical production. If he was nothing else, he was confident.

While Pete retrieved the plywood, Wayne and Tom rolled the four red-and-white striped barrels into position to make the four corners of the stage. It was a construction site, never intended to be used as a dance venue, but Wayne was ingenuous when it came to improvising. The moon was nearly full; no need to light the stage with the headlights of the patrol cars.

When it was set up and had been tested to make sure it was sturdy enough for Jackie to dance on, Wayne motioned her to the front of the makeshift stage, after which he put a hand on each side of her waist and lifted her onto the plywood deck.

"Ok, guys. Jackie is a dancer and a contortionist. Don't call her a stripper. She won't like it. Rookie, get that basket over there and put it on the stage beside her." Wayne pointed at the basket.

As he lifted it onto the stage, Pete Tarleton asked, "What's in the basket?"

"You are all going to love this," Wayne replied. "Jackie has a pet boa constrictor. His name is Studley and he dances with her."

Pete Tarleton dropped the basket onto the stage and backed away, his face a little paler in the moonlight than it had been just moments before.

Jackie was wearing a pair of red shorts and a man's shirt with the tails tied at the bottom of her ribcage. She turned from the five men, pulled two sequined pasties from the shirt's pocket and applied one to the nipple of each breast. The glue from earlier in the night seemed to hold. She then whirled to face the audience. She skillfully slipped from the shirt in a teasing manner before tossing it off the stage into the hands of Wayne Hartman.

Wayne and Billy whooped and laughed as Jackie reached for the zipper on her shorts. She made unbuttoning and unzipping the shorts seem more sensuous than any member of her audience thought possible. Wayne mumbled to himself, "She really is a professional."

As she shimmied out of the shorts, stepping out of one leg, she used the other to toss the shorts into the hands of Tom Bradley. Tom caught the shorts to the sound of Wayne and Billy laughing and whooping again, but becoming a participant in the performance made him uncomfortable. His face reddened as he dropped the shorts onto the ground beside him.

Once the shorts were removed, Jackie was wearing only a G-string with a strip of cloth intended to cover the genitals. Wayne noticed that it was wider and therefore a little less revealing than those most strippers wore. He thought that was probably because Jackie's performance included a variety of contorted positions not taken by most dancers.

Jackie sat on the stage, lifted first one, then the other foot, before placing both behind her neck. She reached for the basket, tossing the lid off, reaching in with one hand to begin coaxing Studley from his resting place. Once the snake was in her hand it began slithering around her arm to her shoulder. Studley was just over five feet long. He began to entwine half its body around and between her legs and then up and around her neck, appearing, for a moment, to be encircling her entire body.

Moments later the snake began to move again, slithering down Jackie's back and onto the stage beside her. Jackie untangled her legs from her neck and lay on her stomach, grasping her ankles behind her back and pulling her legs back, up, and around her neck where she crossed her feet under her chin. She then began to rock slowly on her stomach as the snake again wrapped around her body.

The show continued for 15 minutes before Jackie ended it with a bow, placing the snake back in its basket. The men were mesmerized, mostly by the acrobatics.

After a few minutes of small talk, Jackie said, “I have to get home. I’m scheduled to be back at work at four this afternoon.”

Wayne quickly stepped beside her. “I’ll follow you and make sure you get home alright.”

He turned and winked at the other officers. As he strutted along behind her walking toward her car, he leaned close to Billy Williamson and said, “I’m going to try to get her interested in another snake before she goes back to work.”

With that, the party was over; Wayne and Jackie’s cars were back on the street as the other officers stood close to their patrol cars talking.

“So, rookie, what’d you think of all that?” Billy asked.

“I don’t like snakes and I was worried the entire time that the sergeant might come driving up here. I never thought about doing stuff like this.”

“Well, we work hard when we work and we take a few minutes off on a slow night. With all that we have to deal with out here we need a little relief. You know there’s an old saying that ‘officers don’t get fired for chasing women, drinking or sleeping on duty as long as they answer their calls, don’t get complained on, and get their two arrests a day’ and there’s some truth in that.” Billy said.

Eddie Jackson looked at the rookie. He knew that he was senior only to Pete, but he decided to say what was on his mind.

"Don't listen to Billy and Wayne, kid. They're both too jaded to give you advice about your police career. Working hard and looking for crime is what you signed on to do; so don't let these guys distract you."

As they drove away, Billy said, "Eddie, I really enjoy working with you because you're a real 'go-getter', but when things are slow, you should loosen up."

"Just not the way I am, Billy," was Eddie's only reply.

In the other car, Tom told his rookie, "Eddie's right, you know. Wayne has lots of demons and Billy, well he just goes along. Keep your eye on being a good cop."

"Well if that's true, why did we go out there and meet them then?" Pete questioned.

"None of us are perfect, Pete, but we don't distance ourselves from each other just because we don't agree with everything another cop does. You never know when Wayne or Billy will be the guy who has to pull the fat out of the fire for you one night on a call." Tom said nothing more about the evening's activities.

*****

The following night, when Pete arrived at the substation, he found Eddie, Billy, and Tom in a private conversation in a back corner of the locker room. Seeing Pete, Billy motioned for him to join them. He was pleased to be invited into the veteran officers' circle as he walked over.

"Tom here was about to tell us something about Wayne's dancer from last night." Eddie looked at Pete as he spoke.

Tom began, "Well, I wasn't sure last night, but I checked the name when I got here tonight." The conversation continued in whispered words.

When it ended, the four officers drifted into the roll call room. It was noisy. Several conversations were taking place at the same time as officers congregated in small groups. Wayne was already seated in a far corner and appeared to be reading a bulletin. This struck most of the officers as unusual, since Wayne was typically one of the most boisterous and talkative officers in the room.

But, only four of his co-workers knew the real story. Jackie Sinclair, the dancer with the sensuous moves and body to die for, whom Wayne had followed home the night before, harbored a secret that Wayne Hartman, to his dismay, had also discovered.

Jackie Sinclair was a man!

THE GREEK SAILOR

Grady Henson sat in the roll-call room reading the Houston Chronicle. His shift didn't start until three that afternoon and it was just after two. He had worked an extra job as security for a bank a couple of miles from the Park Place police substation and decided it was better to get to work early than to drive the 15 miles home.

He seethed as he read an investigative reporter's story about the number of shootings Houston police had been involved in for the past two years, especially those working at the Park Place substation. Grady believed the reporter, Harvey Priest, slanted the story to make it sound as if all Houston officers were more interested in shooting citizens than in fighting crime.

When his partner, Tracy Pollard, walked into the room, the two began discussing the story.

"I see you're reading about the murderers in uniform," Tracy began. "Did you notice that Priest didn't even mention the criminal records of those 'victims' who were shot by the police? What a prick, and he calls himself a reporter."

Grady folded the paper. "I did, but what do you expect. All the stories about the times we don't shoot someone wouldn't sell a single newspaper."

An hour later Grady and Tracy were on patrol, answering calls, the newspaper article all but forgotten.

It was a busy afternoon, but by six o'clock they managed to take a meal break at the Tele-Wink Grill. After eating, they wrote a couple of traffic tickets before driving down 75th Street toward the ship channel. It was just after nine; they had two more hours until the end of their shift.

Approaching South Harbor Street, they saw a large black woman and a much smaller white man standing in the middle of the intersection. Both were waving their arms and shouting. Grady pulled the patrol car to the curb and advised the dispatcher they would be out on a disturbance at 75th and South Harbor.

"Officer, get this mother-fucker away from me," the woman said.

Grady recognized her. She was Johnnie Lee Hooker, an appropriate last name, since it also described her occupation.

"Johnnie Lee, what's going on?" Grady asked.

"This mother-fucker thinks he loves me." Johnnie Lee was in rare form. "He got off a ship night before last and I turned a trick with him. Then he came back last night and wanted to do some weird shit. I charged him a little more for last night and now here he is again tonight, half drunk and saying he wants to marry me. Get him the fuck away from me!"

Tracy pulled the sailor a few feet away and began asking questions. He quickly learned that the sailor was Greek and spoke fair, but broken English. The man smelled of whiskey and was a little tipsy, but was coherent. He declared that he was in love with Johnnie Lee and wanted to marry her before his ship sailed. Tracy asked him for some identification and the sailor complied.

At the same time, Grady asked Johnnie Lee for her identification. He got a totally different response.

"What you mean, you want I.D. You know who I am! You supposed to protect me from crazy sailors like this. Why you want to fuck with me?"

With that, Johnnie Lee turned to walk away.

Grady reached for her arm and when he touched her, the fight began. She swung with her right, hitting a glancing blow on the side of his head. Seeing this, Tracy ran to help his partner. In a matter of seconds, Johnnie Lee was handcuffed, but she continued to struggle. Both officers were giving her their undivided attention.

"Let her go! Let her go," the sailor screamed.

Tracy looked back at the sailor and saw that he was about 10 feet away, holding a pistol in both hands, pointing it in the direction of the officers and Johnnie Lee.

"You not put her in jail! She is my wife soon! Get away from her," he continued to scream at the officers, as he waved the pistol wildly.

Grady would have to control Johnnie Lee by himself. Tracy moved away from them and toward the sailor. As he did, he pulled his pistol from its holster and held it beside his leg.

"Easy now, sailor; lower the pistol," Tracy said in a low, calm voice as he continued moving slowly toward the sailor with his left hand extended.

He thought he saw confusion in the irate man's eyes.

"We can work all this out. Just give me the pistol. We don't want anyone to get hurt."

Tracy was within a long reach of the hand that held the weapon. He considered grabbing for it, but decided to continue with a slow, methodical approach.

"You can't put her in jail! My ship sails in two days. Let her go!"

As the sailor spoke, Tracy now noted that his tone of voice was less threatening and sounded tormented with indecision.

Another half-step and Tracy slowly put his hand on the barrel of the pistol. Pushing it to the side, he holstered his own weapon at the same time. Just when he thought it was over, suddenly the sailor began to struggle. But, no match for the much larger officer, in seconds the man was being handcuffed as he lay face down on the pavement.

Grady had already placed Johnnie Lee in the back seat of the patrol car as a small crowd gathered. Two young black men began taunting the officers. As Sergeant Hinkle, who had decided to check by, pulled up to the scene, the sailor was quickly placed into the seat beside the hooker.

"Sarge, let's drive up the street a few blocks and get away from the crowd. We'll fill you in there," Grady said as he got into his patrol car and pulled away.

A few blocks from the crowd of on-lookers, they met the sergeant in a parking lot. Both officers got out of their car. The two prisoners remained in the back seat. Grady explained what had happened to the sergeant, but Tracy suddenly interrupted.

"Oh, shit. I never did shake the guy down. We need to get him out of the car and search him."

Tracy helped the sailor out of the rear seat of the patrol car and began searching him. When he patted the right rear pocket he felt something hard. He reached in and pulled out a red silk handkerchief. It was wrapped around the heavier object, a very small .25 caliber automatic pistol.

"You guys put him in the car without searching him?" The sergeant's question sounded more like an accusation.

"Sarge, you saw that crowd. We needed to get away from there. No harm, no foul; that's the way I see it," Grady said.

"Get him back in the car and take 'em both to jail."

The sergeant turned and walked to his car, clearly not impressed with Grady's explanation.

The next day as the two partners were walking into the roll call room, Grady commented, "Well, partner, I see we didn't make the paper this morning with a story about the officer who DIDN'T shoot the Greek sailor. I was right. It's just not newsworthy."

During roll call, the desk sergeant reminded everyone to search their prisoners thoroughly after making an arrest.

As he finished his roll call duties, he added, "Henson and Pollard, report to the lieutenant's office when we're through here."

A few minutes later, the two officers were advised to prepare written statements explaining their failure to properly search a prisoner. The lieutenant told them he would be recommending that each be suspended for one day without pay as a result of the oversight.

When they had completed the statements and were in their patrol car, Grady looked at Tracy, whose face was filled with anger and frustration.

"It's just the life of a cop, partner. The news media crucifies us for shooting too many crooks! Then you risk your life, and mine, by the way, to keep from shooting a little Greek sailor. All of that topped off with the brass taking their 30 pieces of silver out of our pay checks."

"Yeah, just like the story of Jesus, except the crucifixion takes place first for us."

Tracy reached for the radio to answer their first call of the day.

THE OLD WOMAN

Every cop who worked at the Park Place substation knew the old woman, no matter what shift he worked. She lived off a main road in an old house, so run down it appeared to be vacant. It had tall weeds surrounding it, a sagging gate with a broken hinge, and a roof ready to collapse; one of those houses amateur artists love to paint.

Mrs. Gertrude Baxter was a short woman, hefty, but not much overweight, with grey hair tied in a bun at the back of her head. Her face was tanned and leathery from many years in the harsh Houston sun; the wrinkles of age were well-defined and somewhat becoming on a face that had once been soft and still held a sense of youth. What struck most people were her eyes. They were pale blue, incandescent and appeared bottomless. Even at her advanced age, the eyes directed one's imagination to a young woman, adventurous, intelligent, and living life to its fullest.

She called the police to report various goings on in her neighborhood, if it could even be called a neighborhood. The nearest home was a half mile down the road, with a pasture and a wooded area separating it from her place. Mrs. Baxter was on a list at the dispatcher's office of habitual callers. Not on the "mental case" list, just the list of people who called often for police services. The “mental case” call list was for those truly disturbed people who would meet officers at the door with tin foil wrapped around their heads to ward off extraterrestrials, or insist that aliens were in their attics, or that neighbors were stealing eggs from a refrigerator.

Sergeant Bill Travis had been making calls at Mrs. Baxter’s house since he was a rookie on the night-shift. Bill believed that she was just lonely and enjoyed talking to officers who made the calls, but there was usually some validity to her complaints. Sometimes she reported trespassers on a neighboring pasture or teenagers parked on the deserted road, engaged in either drinking beer or making out, sometimes both.

Once an officer arrived, she never seemed too concerned about those activities. She wanted to talk. If the officer would listen she might tell the story of her husband buying the 500 acres surrounding her home back in 1922. She’d tell how after he died she had sold it off one small parcel at a time until now she only owned five acres and the old house. There were a hundred other stories from a life well-lived; few had heard them all.

Most officers tried to avoid the calls to Mrs. Baxter’s place because it was so difficult to get away. She would offer to fix lunch or a glass of tea; anything to keep the officer there for a few more minutes. Housekeeping was not her strong suite and she kept dozens of cats living inside or roaming outside her home. Those facts alone discouraged most officers from accepting her generosity. But Bill Travis, or Sergeant Bill, as Mrs. Baxter called him, was different. While he never accepted her offer of meals or tea, he always sat on the porch with her a few minutes to listen to the stories of times long past. He probably knew more about Gertrude Baxter than any other living person, simply because he took the time to listen.

Once Mrs. Baxter learned that Sergeant Bill had transferred to the day-shift, she stopped calling the dispatcher and instead called directly to the Park Place station asking for him. If he was in the office, he would take the call and visit by phone, usually negating the need for a patrol car to visit her home. If he was working on the street and got her message, he drove by her home for a visit. He was performing "community-oriented policing" long before the term or the program was introduced in Houston.

Other sergeants laughed at him, joking that he picked his girlfriends a little too old for their taste or that he was angling for an inheritance when she finally died. Despite the jokes, most officers appreciated his efforts simply because it meant they didn't have to make the calls.

One day, while visiting with Sergeant Bill, Mrs. Baxter turned the conversation to her many calls to the police department.

"You know, of course, Sergeant Bill, I am well aware that some of your fellow officers think I'm a senile old woman."

Bill didn't respond, but looked expectantly at the old woman wanting to learn more.

"I'm not senile at all, though. I call when I see things that might be suspicious. I know that most of the time, it's really nothing, but I do so enjoy visiting with you and the other officers. None of my old friends are left and I have little opportunity to talk to other people."

Bill simply nodded his head.

"You know that big metal building on the road behind my property?" Mrs. Baxter lifted her hand and pointed a thumb over her shoulder with the quick change of topics.

"You mean the one that used to be a machine shop?" Bill asked.

"That's the one," she nodded as she reached for a cat rubbing against her leg. "There's something going on there at night and I don't think it's on the up-and-up."

As she lifted the cat onto her lap, Bill leaned back in his chair, "Tell me about it, Mrs. Baxter."

"Well I heard some noise back there one night about a week ago and when I looked out I could see a flame flickering inside the building. I first thought it was on fire and started to call the fire department, but then I saw a truck pull up to the back door and a couple of men got out. I watched for a while and then I couldn't see the flame anymore. A few minutes later the men left.

"Next morning I walked back there and crossed the fence. The chain and padlock that secured the big door on the back of the building was still wrapped through the handles, but it had been cut and wasn't keeping the door shut at all. I walked around to the front and both doors there were still chained shut.

"Nobody came back the next night, but two nights later there was a lot of activity. Three different times I saw men come in and unload something out of the trunks of their cars."

Bill interrupted her, "What were they unloading?"

"Well, it was dark and I didn't get too close, but I saw a television and some boxes they were taking in there. After they left, the truck I saw the first night came back and the fire was back on for a while. I went over there yesterday and went inside. They have two propane burners with little pots setting on top of them and they have been melting something in the pots. One has a yellow color on it and the other looks like silver." The old woman paused for a moment.

"Ok, Mrs. Baxter. I'm going to check it out, but I want you to stay away from there. Whatever is going on, it could be dangerous for you if someone saw you looking around." Bill stood and as he was leaving, told her he would let her know when he learned something.

He drove back to the main road and wound his way around until he was on the street where the building was located. Once there, he pulled to the back to confirm what Mrs. Baxter had told him.

He went inside, where he found the burners and next to them a bucket containing small photos and other paper items that appeared to have been removed from lockets or other jewelry. Walking further into the building, he found several televisions, a few computers, and an assortment of ten rifles and shotguns all piled in a corner. He wrote down serial numbers from what he guessed were the four most expensive weapons and returned to his patrol car.

Bill was sure he had found the base of operations for someone who was buying stolen property. He would check the serial numbers to see if any of the guns had been reported stolen. His friend, a lieutenant in the Burglary and Theft Division, would be interested in this one.

Minutes after returning to the Park Place station, he had confirmed that two of the serial numbers were reported stolen within the last ten days. He called his friend and they met for lunch to develop a plan for surveillance of the building.

Two weeks later, the Department announced the arrest of seventeen individuals for offenses ranging from burglary to selling and buying stolen property. One of the younger burglars, when captured, confessed that he and his friend were burglarizing homes in the more affluent areas of Houston during the day and taking their loot to the old machine shop at night. There they would sort out any jewelry they had stolen into gold, silver, and junk, which they would leave on a table beside the burners. The rest of the bounty was stacked in a corner of the building.

The following day they would go to a local pawn shop where the owner would pay them for the previous night's loot. Each night that the pawn shop owner scheduled his burglar friends to bring property to the building, he and a helper would arrive just after the burglars unloaded the property and left. The two would melt down the jewelry so it couldn't be identified. The owner would then look over the remainder of the new loot and determine what to pay for it. Much of the stolen property would then be sold at his pawn shop to unsuspecting buyers looking for a good deal.

It was a big news story! The police detectives discovered two other warehouses being used for the same purpose. The Burglary and Theft

Division estimated that the recovered property had a value of over two million dollars.

At the annual awards banquet, Sergeant Bill Travis received the “Officer of the Year” award for his work on developing the information leading to the arrests and recovery of property. He was given a Rolex watch engraved on the back with information about the award.

When he stood before the audience to accept the award, he simply said, “I could not have accomplished what I did, if not for the support and assistance of a beautiful woman with beautiful blue eyes. Thank you!”

Those in attendance assumed he was referring to his wife and turned to look at her, seated at a table to the left of the small stage. But sitting next to his wife was an elderly woman, whose pale blue eyes sparkled as she smiled at Sergeant Bill.

THE NAKED GREEN MAN & OTHER COLORFUL TALES

They sat at a long table in the meeting room of a local hamburger joint. Most of them were over sixty. It was a meeting of the Southeast Lunch Bunch. They had all worked at the Houston Police Department's Park Place substation. The monthly meetings were a tradition which began as a way to keep in touch and tell war stories of days long passed. They remained a tight-knit group.

The Naked Green Man

"Any of you guys remember the naked green man?" Mike asked the group. "Before we figured out who he was we'd get calls from neighbors about a naked man painted green who was running up and down the street.

"This went on for about two weeks before one day a neighbor waved us down and told us he'd seen the green man go in a house just down the block.

"We went to the house. No one would answer the door, so we went in the back yard."

Mike told how he and his partner looked through the kitchen window and saw the walls were painted green. There was a big cat, painted the same shade of green, tip-toeing along the counter by the sink.

"Just as we were about to turn away, the green man popped out from behind the door inside the house. He took one look at my partner, Frank, who had been a professional wrestler before becoming a police officer and had the cauliflower ears to prove it.

"The Green Man snarled at Frank, 'What are you looking at, Mickey Mouse ears?' Frank bristled at the remark, his face and ears turning a bright crimson.

"Of course we couldn't go in the house without a warrant, but we drove back down the street fifteen minutes later and the green man was sitting on the curb, wearing nothing but a pair of blue jean shorts. He had a butcher knife in his hand, but jumped up and tried to run when we approached. Luckily, I was able to tackle him and, other than a cut on my wrist, there was no harm.

"We sent him to the county hospital for a mental evaluation. It was the last time there was a report of a naked green man in the neighborhood, but I've still got the scar on my wrist," Mike said as he held his arm up to show the scar.

The Case of the Troublesome Cap

"How about the time Glenn and Ed were riding together and Glenn threw Ed's uniform cap out of the car?" said Ray from the far end of the room.

Both Glenn and Ed had been Marines who, to the surprise of some, didn't like riding together. Glenn, as the story goes, always wore his uniform cap in the patrol car while Ed kept his on the seat between them.

One night when Glenn was driving, they got involved in a chase. He grabbed the 'mic' and was giving locations to the dispatch. He'd toss the 'mic' on the seat to make turns and when he'd pick it up again it would get tangled in Ed's cap.

"So they're chasing this car through a neighborhood and Glenn is yelling at Ed to move his cap. Ed ignores him, probably because he was hanging on for dear life." Ray says. "Finally, Glenn grabs for the 'mic' once more, and again it is tangled up in Ed's cap. He drops the 'mic', grabs the cap, and tosses it out the window.

"Ed begins screaming, 'Stop the car. What are you doing?' but Glenn continues the chase and they eventually catch the guy.

"By the time they got back to the street where the cap was thrown out, it was long gone. Probably a souvenir hung on the wall in some teenager's bedroom along with a stop sign or two."

Black Coffee and Plenty of it

The story prompted another round of laughter, after which Jack spoke up.

"That was before my time, but I remember Glenn. He was my first training officer. Everyone called him 'Pops'."

Ray interrupted, "You know, they gave him that nickname after I left Park Place, but I always thought it was disrespectful, like they were putting him down."

Jack continued, "I'm not sure, Ray, how the nickname came about, but he never seemed to mind, unless you were a rookie; I wouldn't have dared call him anything but 'sir'. You know, my first night on the street, I was just 19 years old. Never drank coffee before that night.

"Glenn pulled into the Shipley Donut drive-thru window at South Park and Loop 610. Black guy by the name of Herman ran it. Glenn held up two fingers and said 'Two coffees, black.' As Herman turned to fill the order I told Glenn that I didn't drink coffee. Big mistake!

"Glenn wasted no time, 'You're a night-shift Park Place Ranger. You drink coffee, and you drink it black.'

"I've drunk it ever since that night. Always black."

A Death Too Soon

Pockets of conversation began to develop around the table, until Ray started speaking again.

"You know we can't tell war stories without at least one about Ronnie. He died too young, but he left us a lot of memories."

"He was in the same cadet class as me, Class 35," Larry said. "We showed up for our last interview before being hired on the same day. Ronnie had ridden a bus from Arkansas and arrived early that morning. After the interviews, the lieutenant asked him what time his bus left to go home. Ronnie said it would be early the next morning.

"The lieutenant offered Ronnie a ride to his hotel, but was shocked when Ronnie said he'd just sleep at the bus station. I think they made some other arrangements for him. He had a lot to learn about the big city."

"He loved being a policeman," Ray said, "You know he used to give free haircuts to the kids at his extra job in the housing projects. He also donated half of what he made there to a fund to pay for organized activities for those kids."

"Yeah, but he could also be merciless with the crooks he caught," Jimmy added. "I remember he carried a bullwhip for a while. One night we caught a burglar crawling out a jewelry store window, but we lost his partner who ran as we were pulling up. Ronnie asked the one we caught what his partner's name was, but the guy just sneered at us and wouldn't talk.

"Ronnie got that whip out and cracked it a couple of times right at the guy's feet. When he still wouldn't talk, Ronnie turned to me and said, 'Take his shirt off, partner.' As I started walking toward him, the burglar gave us the name and address of his buddy. We picked him up on the way to town."

Mike stared at the table. "I wouldn't have been surprised to hear that he was shot by a burglar or while arresting a hi-jacker, but I'd have never thought of him being run down by a drunk out on the freeway. He was a guy that won't easily be forgotten."

The table was silent for a moment, before a waiter interrupted with offers of refilling tea and water glasses.

Shopping Cart Races

Finally, Roger spoke. "One more story before I leave. You guys remember the shopping cart races we used to have at Gulf Gate Mall?"

Several chuckled and nodded their heads. One of the younger guys, with a quizzical look, said he guessed he'd missed that party.

"Well, you know it used to get pretty boring on the night-shift, late Sunday night into the early morning hours of Monday especially. One night Bobby and Speedy were parked at the mall writing a report. One of them came up with a brilliant idea.

"There were usually several shopping carts left on the lot at the end of the day. So Bobby and Speedy drove up to one of the carts, just touching the car bumper to the back of the cart. Then they slowly drove forward, picking up speed until they hit about 25 miles per hour. They backed off and watched the cart sail out of control, wobbling from side to side until finally it tipped over and skidded to a stop in the middle of the lot.

"Of course this was so much fun that before long there were two other patrol cars on the lot with them, and soon they had created a contest to see who could get a cart going fastest before it tipped over. It became a Sunday night ritual for a while. The fastest I knew of was 36 mph. Speedy set that record just minutes before Ben gave it a try and wrapped one of the carts up underneath the front end of his patrol car. That ended the races.

"As I recall, Ben got a day off for damage to the patrol car, but the sergeant never knew what really happened. Ben's story was that he was chasing a speeder who cut across the Gulf Gate Mall parking lot and he accidentally ran over the cart, causing him to lose the speeder."

Roger stood, preparing to leave, while most of the others laughed and started more conversations about the shopping cart escapade.

"You know I feel for these guys who are out there now patrolling the streets," Mike said. "What with all the dash cameras, GPS systems, and other ways of watching them, it's just not like it used to be. I couldn't work out there now."

Baloney! You'd all do it again!

For the first time, Joe decided to contribute to the conversation.

"I came on in 1966 and my first training partner just told me two things the whole month I rode with him.

"First thing he said was, 'No matter what happens out here, you and me get our stories straight before we talk to anybody else, and we take that story to the grave.'

"Second thing he told me was, 'It ain't like it used to be. We used to have a lot of fun out here, but not anymore.' That was Dan Spurling and he'd been on 20 years then.

"I was telling rookies the same thing before I retired and two generations of cops since have repeated it. The fact is it's different for every generation as they adapt to new rules, new laws, more technology, and a public that views them differently than they viewed Dan Spurling when he started in 1946.

"But there's one thing that's never changed. Police work is just pure fun and I'll bet you'd all jump right back in if you were as young and dumb as you were then. See you next month."

MISPLACED GUILT & DEADLY RUMORS

Danny Jackson and Bill Hunter rarely rode together, although they both had worked night-shift at the Park Place police substation for several years. Bill was Mark Moretti's regular partner and they were like brothers. It was rare, even off-duty, to see one without the other. Their families were also close; they even bought houses on the same street. But this month, Moretti was assigned to ride with a rookie. So Bill and Danny were paired together tonight for the first time in months.

Shortly after hitting the streets, the calls for service began rolling in. Their first was a family disturbance call which was settled before they arrived. Next was a prowler call, then a silent burglar alarm. And so it went, call after call, until nearly two in the morning.

Some described Danny as hyperactive; others just said he was born with ants in his pants. He was easily bored and rarely took advantage of the short stretches of calm to recharge for the next burst of activity. A few officers, including Moretti, didn't like riding with him for that reason. If he wasn't responding to a call, he was likely to be trolling the freeway, looking for drunks and speeders. He had to be doing something!

So when the calls slowed down that night, he suggested to Bill that they try to catch a speeder on the Gulf Freeway. As they entered the freeway ramp from Park Place Boulevard to head north, a "whistler" passed them by without slowing down. A car traveling at high speed creates a sound similar to whistling. Officers encountering one of these might advise the dispatcher that he was chasing a "whistler." Bill and Danny began the chase.

Nearly a mile down the road they turned on the emergency red lights and siren. It took several seconds for the driver to realize he was being chased by a police car, at which time he braked and pulled to the side of the freeway. Danny exited the car and walked to the driver's door. He asked to see the driver's license, but barely had the request out of his mouth when Bill yelled at him.

"Partner, let's go! Robbery in progress at the Exxon station, Wayside and the freeway."

Danny glanced at the driver. "This is your lucky night. Slow down," he said, as he turned and raced back to the patrol car.

The officers, just blocks from the robbery, turned off the red lights as they sped by the relieved driver and took the Wayside exit. They drove beside the service station and Bill jumped from the still rolling car, circling to the back of the building. As he rounded the corner he was met by a black man who raised a .45 caliber automatic pistol and fired one time directly into Bill's face. He fell, dying before his body hit the ground.

The suspect, later identified as Leroy Smallwood, had seen the police car as it approached. He knew there were two officers, but didn't see where the other one went, so he ran toward the freeway and sprinted up the embankment to the southbound lanes of the roadway. Just then, Mark Moretti and his rookie, Johnny Parker, arrived at the scene and abandoned their police car in the middle of the street to give chase on foot.

Danny, having heard the shot, but not knowing that it had killed his partner, was in hot foot pursuit of the suspect. He stopped to fire several shots as Smallwood began the ascent toward the main lanes of freeway traffic. One bullet ricocheted off the concrete curb and struck the overhead lights on Moretti's cruiser. Smallwood was wounded, but managed to reach the center median between the lanes of traffic where he collapsed.

As Moretti, Parker, and Danny dodged traffic and ran toward Smallwood, he struggled to his feet and attempted to run. Moretti fired, hitting him multiple times before his pistol was emptied. Leroy Smallwood lay dead in the middle of the freeway, his blood oozing into the cracked concrete.

More officers converged on the frantic scene. Even though the officers knew Bill Hunter was beyond medical help, homicide detectives instructed the ambulance drivers to take him to Ben Taub Hospital.

When Parker McKnight arrived at work the following morning, most of the night-shift crew was still in the report room. McKnight soon learned what had happened to Bill Hunter and McKnight's academy classmate, Danny Jackson.

As the officers discussed the events of the night, Moretti, obviously distraught, spoke.

"Bill wasn't killed by that guy. Jackson shot him accidentally. That son-of-a-bitch has no business on the police department."

Surprised, McKnight looked around the room. Most of the officers were looking at the floor or otherwise trying to avoid eye contact.

"Moretti, are you sure about that? Were you guys on the scene when it happened?" McKnight asked.

"I didn't have to be there. I know what an idiot Jackson is. Hell, he shot up our patrol car when we arrived. I should never have let Bill ride with him," Moretti was raging out of control.

The officers began to drift out of the room, most headed for home, glad to be away from Moretti's outburst. McKnight stopped Wayne Hartman.

"Is there anything to what Moretti is saying?" he asked.

Wayne responded in the cocksure way he usually spoke. "Probably nothing to it; Moretti just hasn't come to grips with losing his buddy. He'll blow off some steam and it'll all be over."

"That's not the kind of accusation Danny needs to deal with right now if it's not based on facts." McKnight turned to go to roll-call.

The days following Bill's death were a nightmare for Danny Jackson. When he attended a gathering at the funeral home the night before the funeral, he collapsed as he viewed the body of Bill Hunter. The next day at the funeral, Bill's death continued to devastate Danny and he was unable to walk without assistance.

But life moves on. Although still deeply troubled, Danny returned to work. Then, within a month of the shooting, the rumor that Moretti had started the morning of the shooting began to circulate. Did Leroy Smallwood really kill Bill Hunter or did Danny Jackson shoot him by mistake?

Moretti, still angry at the world because of his friend's death, never retracted his original accusation. He would simply say, "Well, Jackson did shoot up my patrol car that night. He's hyper. Who knows what happened out there."

The police culture is a breeding ground for baseless rumor, and this one continued to circulate, despite all the evidence confirming that Smallwood was the shooter. As a result, over the next year, the story became an oft repeated myth. Even cadets in the police academy heard the story about the officer who accidentally shot his partner.

Nearly two years after the shooting, Danny, who had asked to be assigned desk duty, was approached by a rookie who innocently inquired if he was around when the officer was killed by his partner. Danny stared at him for a moment, trying to decide if the rookie knew who he was talking to.

Realizing the man was clueless; he ignored the question, turned his back, and feigned to be busy shuffling papers. A few minutes later, the rookie’s training officer guided him from the desk and told him that Danny Jackson was that partner.

Danny studied for promotion to detective while working the desk assignment and was soon promoted. Most officers thought he requested the desk assignment in order to study, but he confided to his former academy friend, Parker McKnight, that he would never work with a partner again. He told McKnight he didn’t want to get another officer killed. His friend tried to reason with him, but Danny remained resolute.

After promotion, he was assigned to the Burglary and Theft Division. He quickly made a name as an aggressive investigator who worked constantly. Although a policy required detectives to work in pairs when serving warrants, Danny received informal counseling twice for failing to do so.

The department changed a few years after Bill was killed. A Psychological Services Division was created. Officers involved in a shooting must be debriefed and are given counseling when needed. When the service was implemented, there was no requirement that officers previously involved in such situations be screened for Post-Traumatic Stress Disorder. Danny remained a haunted and troubled man because of the death of Bill amplified by the rumor that, although not as prolific as it had once been, still circulated.

One day while working in the office, making phone calls to witnesses on his cases, Danny answered a phone call from a person who refused to identify himself. The caller said simply that Harmon Barclay was wanted by the Houston police and at that moment, was located in an apartment project on Richmond Avenue. The caller gave the number of the apartment. Upon checking, Danny found that Harmon Barclay was, indeed, wanted on a warrant for robbery.

Many detectives, upon receiving such information, would simply call the Robbery Division and pass it on to the detective assigned the case, but not Danny Jackson. This was an opportunity to get out of the office and engage in real police work. He didn't even consider asking someone to ride with him.

Upon arriving at the address of the apartment project and just before exiting his car, he called the dispatcher and advised that he was executing an arrest warrant. He asked for a uniformed unit to check by. He then proceeded into the apartment courtyard without waiting for his back-up.

As he walked into the area of the swimming pool, a man lounging by the pool in a reclining deck chair saw him and jumped to his feet. The man ran into an apartment directly behind the chair he had just abandoned. It was the apartment number given by the anonymous caller.

Within seconds, the door burst open and the man calmly walked through the door blasting away with a 12-gauge shotgun held in both hands. Danny Jackson, hit three times in the torso, stumbled back into the swimming pool. He will never again face the sleepless nights, the misplaced guilt, nor will he be tormented by the death of Bill Hunter.

THE PROWLER CALL

Tom Bradley and Billy Williamson had requested to be partners on the night-shift at the Park Place substation. Having ridden together sporadically for over a year, they had decided that their policing styles were similar. With the same days off, it was a full-time partnership.

By midnight one Thursday they had handled two calls, one a prowler and the other a family disturbance. After quickly resolving both, Billy drove toward the Dot Shop, an all-night diner on the Gulf Freeway. The food there was passable and the manager gave officers half off the menu price.

Since the robbery of another all-night diner two years ago, during which the manager was shot and killed, restaurants in the area tried to attract officers, by reducing menu prices by half. A police presence amounted to cheap security in the wee hours of the morning.

They had just turned onto the service road a hundred feet from the Dot, when the call came in.

"Unit 732, make the prowler call at 6800 Ilex Street."

Billy picked up the 'mic' and acknowledged that they received the call.

"Well, I guess we'll wait a little later to eat," Tom commented. "At least a prowler call isn't likely to keep us tied up for very long."

Billy turned onto Ilex Street as Tom looked for house numbers using his handheld spotlight.

"Here it is, Partner, on the right," Tom said, dropping the spotlight on the seat and reaching for the door handle.

Both officers left the car. Tom being closest to the curb was first to walk up the driveway. Seconds later a man stepped from the garage behind the house and walked toward them. It was dark, but in the sliver of moonlight that sliced across the driveway, Tom saw the man's hands wrapped around either a rifle or shotgun.

It was not unusual for an armed homeowner to meet officers responding to a prowler call, but Tom sensed that something wasn't right. For years after that night, he could never quite put his finger on why. He just knew it wasn't right.

Tom directed the beam of his flashlight at the man's face. "Hold up, my friend," he commanded.

In one swift motion, the man looked directly at Tom, placed the barrel of the weapon in his mouth, holding it with his left hand. Staring wide-eyed at Tom, he reached down with his right and pulled the trigger. His body lifted slightly off the ground and then collapsed onto the concrete.

The shot jolted Tom. Inching closer, he saw that half the man's head was gone, from the upper jaw, back to his left ear.

"This son-of-a-bitch just shot himself!" Tom swore as Billy stepped past him.

"No shit!" Billy kicked the weapon away from the dead body, as if there might still be a danger.

Seconds later the front door to the house opened a few inches. An attractive woman, in her thirties, peeked out.

"Did you see him? I heard a shot," she asked, glancing tentatively from side to side.

"Yes, Ma'am, we saw him. He shot himself," Billy responded. "Shot his head nearly off."

The woman began screaming immediately and collapsed in the doorway of the house. A second woman flung the door wide-open and knelt to assist her, staring at the officers.

"He's her husband," she said. "They've been separated and he came over, beat on the door and tried to come in. She told me to call the police. He said they'd never take him back to jail.

"I'm her sister. I need to call our family doctor. He's been treating her for depression since the separation."

The doctor, a family friend who lived only six blocks away, arrived at the home fifteen minutes later. He treated the wife with a sedative as Tom gathered information from the sister.

When a death is involved, the responding patrol officer is expected to advise the Homicide office. Detectives are usually assigned to the scene in order to complete the report. Tom located the phone, dialed the Homicide office and asked to speak to the lieutenant.

"Lieutenant Kirtley."

"Lieutenant, this is Tom Bradley. We responded to a prowler call on Ilex Street. When we arrived, the prowler met us on the driveway and blew his head off with a shotgun. Sounded like a small caliber rifle, but it's a 12-gauge."

Tom kept his voice low to avoid more emotional outbursts from the family.

The lieutenant burst into laughter. "I bet it did sound like a pop gun. A man's head makes a hell of a silencer."

Tom heard as the lieutenant began to speak to someone in the office with him. "Get on the other line. You're not going to believe this." He then resumed talking to Tom.

"My God! Sum'bitch just shot hisself when you shined your light on him. That's a new one for me," the lieutenant guffawed, trying to gain control of his laughter.

After Tom filled him in on the remaining details of the incident, he asked, "Lieutenant, you sending a team of detectives out for this one?"

"Hell, no, Bradley. Who could do the reports on a suicide better than the officer that witnessed it?" The lieutenant began chortling again before he hung up the phone.

Tom hung up and turned to his partner.

"Well, Billy, looks like we'll miss that visit to the Dot. We'll be doing the paperwork on this one."

After turning the scene in the driveway over to the medical examiner's investigator, the two officers went back into the house. The wife, still gaining control of her emotions, sat at the kitchen table with her sister and the doctor.

Billy looked at the sister, "Didn't you tell me there were a couple of kids asleep in the bedroom?"

"Yes, I did, officer. My sister's two boys; they don't know about their daddy. They've slept through all of this. They're just four and five years old," the sister responded.

"Well, before they wake up in the morning, be sure somebody goes out and cleans up around where the body was. There's blood, brains, and bones all over the driveway. They don't need to see that," Billy said.

The words, cold and hard, triggered another anguished scream from the wife. The sister and the doctor glared at Billy with disgust. Tom grabbed Billy's arm and pulled him toward the door.

Once in the car, Tom looked at his partner, his face a mask of confusion.

"Man, why'd you say that in front of the wife? That wasn't necessary."

"What do you mean, Tom? I was just trying to protect those kids," said Billy, oblivious to the havoc his ill-considered words caused. "Let's go by the Dot for some breakfast before we start the paperwork, Tom. I could use some scrambled eggs with chili on top. That'll remind me what the guy's head looked like. Sure wouldn't be my preferred method of killing myself, not that I would consider it anyway."

Tom sat quietly as they drove back toward the freeway. Both officers had been desensitized to scenes of violence since early in their careers. Older officers enjoyed taking rookies to gruesome scenes just to get the reaction of the neophytes.

While Tom showed no emotion, Billy dealt with witnessing a man kill himself with bravado and sick humor, intent on proving he wasn't affected by human tragedy. Although each man coped with it in his own manner, like nearly all officers, they both met the need to compartmentalize their emotions when dealing with such matters.

THE CHASE

Pete Tarleton and Johnny Parker were assigned to patrol the quietest district in southeast Houston. District 14 included the largely undeveloped land at Houston's southern border. To the east, it bordered the Pasadena city limits. Driving south on Interstate 45, known as the Gulf Freeway, the next city, several miles outside Houston's city limits, was Webster. It was a small community destined, in a few years, to grow tremendously because of the influx of businesses related to NASA and a burgeoning healthcare industry expanding inland from Galveston Island.

Pete and Johnny enjoyed riding together, but tonight they would have preferred an assignment with more action. Neither had been on the department quite four years. They had both requested assignment to the Park Place police substation simply because they knew, for the most part, it was a busy area with lots of action.

The first stop of the night was at a service station located just off the freeway. That's where Jack Rush worked the night-shift at the only all night gas stop in the district.

Like most businesses that stayed open all night, Jack encouraged the police to drop by for an added sense of security in the wee hours of the morning. But he also genuinely enjoyed talking to the officers who worked the area.

He always had fresh coffee ready and kept a police scanner radio turned on inside the station, so officers could leave their vehicle without missing a police call. It would be four more years before Houston patrol officers carried hand-held radios.

"You guys were just a couple of minutes late," Jack began as the two officers prepared coffee. "There was a whistler just went by that nearly blew the window out. He must have been doing at least 120." As usual, Jack used cop terminology for a fast-moving car on the freeway.

Pete smiled. Jack always enjoyed telling them about the speeder they just missed, the suspicious looking guy who had stopped just to air up a tire, or a customer who looked exactly like the bank robber whose photo was shown on the 10 o'clock news earlier that night. Most officers who knew him assumed that Jack embellished those stories, but they considered it harmless.

"Well, we can't catch all of them, Jack, but we'll keep trying," he said, taking a sip of coffee.

The officers knew that Jack's wife was an invalid. She had been involved in an auto accident years before. A spinal injury had confined her to a wheelchair since. Jack worked the night-shift so he could help her during the day. He didn't make much money and the officers admired his commitment to his family. They were happy to indulge the colorful stories regarding the crimes and misdemeanors he observed at the often lonely location of the service station.

"I may have told you about being robbed a couple of years ago. The guy pulled a pistol on me as soon as I walked out to his car. I got a really good description though. Never could figure why they didn't catch the guy." Jack had told both officers this story several times.

As robberies go, it had been routine. The police report, however, indicated that when the officer arrived on the scene, it was several minutes before Jack gained control of his emotions enough to tell the officer what happened. Pete and Johnny suspected the description might not have been quite as detailed as Jack remembered, contributing to why the case was never solved.

As the two officers finished their coffee, Johnny asked, "Jack, how's your wife doing?"

It was a nightly ritual, and Jack appreciated the inquiry.

"She's doing about the same. You know, of course, she'll never get out of that wheelchair." Jack replied. "But she's got an attitude that is hard to believe. She's always smiling.

"Let us know if we can give you a hand with anything." Pete added. "I guess we better get back to work. We'll drop by again before our shift ends."

Back in the car, Johnny commented, “You know that radio has been silent ever since we hit the road. This is going to be one boring night.”

“Why don’t we head down toward Webster and see if Jamison is working tonight?” Pete suggested. “I’d like to see if he’ll play on our softball team again this year.”

Russ Jamison was a Webster police officer and star softball player.

“Yeah, it’s probably safe to sneak out of the district for a while,” Johnny said cautiously. “Sergeant Collier is working Park Place alone tonight, and he’ll stay in the station working crossword puzzles. I worry a little though, because of those two guys working downtown who were suspended for a day without pay last month after they were caught outside their district.”

They drove south on the freeway and took the City of Webster exit. Pete spotted a pay phone in a strip shopping center, about three blocks from the freeway. The businesses in the center were all closed. Johnny got out of the car, walked to the pay phone, and called the Webster police dispatcher.

“Webster Police. This is Johnson. How can I help you?”

Pete knew Pam Johnson. She’d been dispatching on the night-shift for Webster longer than he had been an officer.

"Hey, Pam, Pete Tarleton. Can you have Russ meet me at the freeway exit? I need to visit with him."

The Houston Police Department did not share radio frequencies with other agencies, necessitating the phone call. But Pete trusted Pam. She knew that the rules were bent from time to time. She wouldn't be the one to snitch on Pete and Johnny for driving to Webster, and risking a day off without pay for leaving their district.

"I'll get the message to him," she said.

Pete turned out of the parking lot heading back to the freeway. There was a small gravel parking lot on the corner where road crews dumped gravel for use in road repair. The officers pulled into the lot and waited only a few minutes before the Webster police car pulled in.

"Hey, guys," Russ Jamison said as he pulled to a stop beside them. "You know your rear driver's side tire is nearly flat?"

The look on Pete's face telegraphed his concern, which was evident in what he was about to say.

"Oh, shit! Tell me you're kidding, please," he said, staring at Jamison.

"Sorry, Pete, but it's flat. I'll help you guys change it," Jamison responded.

"The problem is that we don't carry spare tires. We have to call a city tire-service truck. It's going to be difficult to explain why we're way out here instead of in our district."

"Only HPD would give a guy a car with no spare tire." Russ chuckled as he spoke.

"That's right, Russ," Johnny responded. "But it's a little different buying four or five spare tires at Webster P.D. and paying for 1,500 of them in Houston. It's all about saving the taxpayer money."

Pete was worried. He didn't want to talk about which agency had the best spare tire policy.

"There are only two reasons for us to be down here. One is if we were dispatched to come down here and the other is if we chased a suspect this far south. I don't know what we're going to do." Pete looked at Johnny as if he might have a solution.

Johnny wasted no time deciding what to do.

"Russ, can you give me a ride up the freeway to the Hobby Airport exit? I'll have Wayne Hartman meet us there. I think I know how we can fix this."

After a short discussion, during which Johnny explained his plan, he lifted the radio microphone from its clip on the dashboard and called for Hartman to meet them in fifteen minutes. He then got into the car with Russ Jamison, leaving Pete to wait with the disabled police cruiser.

A few minutes later, Johnny was sitting in Wayne Harman's patrol car explaining what had happened. Wayne thought it was funny that the two younger officers had put themselves in such a fix but he agreed to help.

"Of course if I do this, you guys are going to owe me big time," he said.

Johnny acknowledged by shaking his head. He got out of the car, thanked Russ Jamison, and told him they would give him a few minutes to get back to Webster before initiating their plan.

Fifteen minutes later Wayne pulled his patrol car onto the service road and headed south. The freeway was deserted, not a headlight nor a taillight in either direction. As they entered the freeway, he turned on the siren.

Johnny reached for the microphone and identified himself with the radio call number.

"743, we've got one running from us, south on the Gulf Freeway approaching Airport. It's a small dark colored sports car."

The dispatcher acknowledged the chase and advised all other units to stay off the radio except for emergencies.

Johnny continued to relay locations by identifying cross streets. His third radio transmission included, "He's pulling away from us. We can't get the license number."

The reports continued until they approached the Webster exit.

"743, he's exited the freeway and heading into Webster at about 90 miles an hour. Hold on."

As Wayne turned off the siren and pulled up beside Pete in the patrol car with the flat tire, Johnny was on the radio again.

"743, we had a flat tire coming off the freeway. We lost him. We'll be at the Webster exit, waiting for a tire truck."

Wayne Hartman then took the microphone and advised that he was just behind the other unit and would try to find the sports car. All three got out of their cars as Russ Jamison pulled to a stop. There were high-fives all around as they chuckled at their clever scheme.

By the time the city tire truck arrived and changed the flat tire it was nearly 4:30 in the morning. Wayne had long since returned to his district and Russ to patrolling his city. As they reached the Houston city limits, Johnny suggested they stop by Jack's service station and have another cup of coffee as they killed time waiting for the shift to end.

"Man, I saw that sports car. It was a dark green Mustang! Must have been doing 130 when he flew by on the freeway! You guys lost him, huh?" Jack was excited.

"Yeah, Jack we lost him in Webster. You think it was a green Mustang?" Pete turned to pour coffee and to conceal his smile.

"Oh, I don't think it was a Mustang! I know it was! In fact, I think it was that kid, Jack Turner. You know he just got a new Mustang last week. I'll bet if you go by his house, the car is still hot from the chase." Jack couldn't contain his enthusiasm.

"Well, Jack, I think we've had enough excitement for tonight. We'll just have to chalk this one up to the bad guys winning one."

After finishing their coffee, when they were driving toward the station to end the shift, Johnny looked at Pete.

"You know, of course, that we could never use what he tells us as reliable information in a criminal case. His imagination is just too vivid. I guess he imagined the red emergency lights that we never turned on, too."

"Sure I know that," Pete replied, "but he's a great witness if the sergeant gets suspicious about our little chase into Webster. Besides, he'll have a hell of a story to tell his wife today. It'll probably get better as the day goes on and he will have caught the green Mustang himself."

CHANGING TIMES

That night, in 1971, as Hal Brock drove to work, he was thinking about his job. There was an academy class graduating and the rookies would get their first assignments as real Houston cops. This class had already made the news. Among the forty-eight cadets who would be graduating, eleven were African American, more diversity than any previous class. Not yet reported in the news, was a rumor that those black rookie officers assigned to the night-shift would ride with white officers. That had never happened before either!

When Hal first came to the Houston P.D., in 1966, the only two blacks working night-shift were assigned to the main police station on Riesner Street. He could remember the two, Turner and Massey, sitting at the back of the roll-call room alone. He never saw them talk to other officers. Their beat was what was known as the "third ward," an area around Dowling Street, one of the roughest black areas in Houston. Hal had only spent a month working at the central station. He hadn't seen them since being assigned to Park Place seven years earlier.

Concerns about whether one of the black officers would be assigned to Park Place where he would ride with a white officer were openly discussed in the locker room and at roll-call. Woody Stinson, a veteran cop of 16 years, said flat out that he would quit the department before riding with a black, although that's not the term he used. Others voiced similar sentiments about riding with blacks, but most didn't draw the line in the sand threatening to end their careers.

Hal wasn't sure integrating patrol cars was as bad as others thought it might be. He had grown up in the midwest where racism was also a fact of life, but the venomous racial talk that he heard here in Houston was new to him. If he was assigned to ride with a black officer, he guessed he would do as he was told.

Hal pulled into the parking lot and parked behind the substation. As he entered the building, he realized that he had barely made it on time. Most of his shift was already seated in the roll-call room; Sergeant Calhoun was standing in front of the podium organizing papers. Hal slipped into a seat on the back row.

Calhoun was an 'old school' sergeant. He had been with the department for 34 years, was an unrepentant and vocal racist, who also believed a woman's place was in the kitchen or the bedroom. Once, when an elderly black man came to the substation to report an auto accident, he made the mistake of not removing his hat when he approached the desk. Sergeant Calhoun had berated him with his booming voice as officers waiting for roll call stood uncomfortably and watched.

"Nigger, don't you have any manners? Don't you know you don't come in MY police station wearing your hat?"

The man had simply removed his hat, looked down and said, "Yes, suh. Sorry, suh."

Calhoun began the early shift roll call. The night-shift was divided into two sub-shifts. About half of the officers started at 10 and the other half at 11. This allowed for an overlap at the beginning and end of each shift. Hal saw that Tom Bradley, who normally reported at 11, was seated at a table beside the podium.

"Listen up," Sergeant Calhoun slammed his clipboard down on the podium. "I had Bradley come in early tonight to represent the late shift. No way to sugar-coat it. We got one of the niggers assigned out here starting tomorrow night. Somebody's going to have to ride with him. I want to be fair, so we'll cut cards to see whether he goes early or late shift. High card wins. Jackson, get up here and draw a card for the early shift."

The sergeant spread a deck of cards on the table in front of Tom Bradley. Bradley and Eddie Jackson each removed a card. Eddie flipped his over to show a five of diamonds. When Bradley turned his card, a groaning sound spread throughout the room. It was the ace of spades.

"Alright, he's going to be on the early shift. Now we'll draw cards to see who rides with him."

The sergeant gathered the cards, shuffled them and laid the deck back on the table. "Form a line and get your card."

In less than two minutes everyone had a card. Bobby Joiner's was the three of diamonds, the lowest card drawn. There was little joking as the men left the room. To a few of the older officers, it was the worst experience they could imagine. To most, however, it was just a reflection of how the rest of society was changing. The police social structure always seemed to lag behind in adjusting to such matters.

On the way to the locker room, Hal put his hand on Bobby's shoulder and asked, "Are you okay with this?"

"Sure, I'm alright. I knew this was coming, so I took several days off this month just in case I drew the low card. I can ride with him, but I intend to see that some of the rest of you do too," Bobby responded.

As Bobby drove to the station the next night, he thought about how everyone was reacting to this change. He didn't have strong feelings about riding with a black cop, but knew that his buddies expected him to show some degree of righteous indignation at the evolving racial tolerance taking place within the police department. Using a few vacation days throughout the next month would let everyone on the shift know that he wasn't too happy about being the first to ride with a black.

When he walked into the roll-call room, he saw a young black officer seated about four rows from the front. No other officers sat within five chairs in any direction. Bobby took a seat on the back row.

The sergeant called out the night's assignments. "Joiner, you'll be riding unit 724 with your rookie, Young."

So there it was. Although he usually rode in district thirteen, primarily a white area, while he was with the rookie he'd be assigned to district twelve. That was the Sunnyside area, a black community. He guessed that even while the racial barrier was being broken inside police cars, the sergeant wasn't quite ready to impose the same standard out in the community.

As they loaded their gear, Bobby looked over the top of the car and asked, "What's your first name?"

"It's James," the rookie responded without looking at his partner.

Once in the car, Bobby extended his hand to shake with his new partner, "Call me Bobby."

As the two men shook hands, Bobby continued, "Let's get this out of the way before we leave the parking lot. I guess you know you'll be the first black cop to ride with a white on the night-shift. Most of the guys out here aren't racists, but they don't like change, so it's going to be rough for a while. All I expect is that if we run into a problem out here on the streets, you'll always have my back."

James stared at Bobby for a moment, trying to decide if he was making a joke. Did he really believe that most of the guys who had just left roll call were not racist? Well, maybe he and his partner had different understandings of what racism was!

James stared straight ahead as he spoke. "Officer Joiner, I just want to learn to be a good cop. You tell me what to do and I'm with you. I'm not asking you to like me, just to teach me."

"Well, you can start by calling me by my first name. Black or white, we're partners. If you want to be accepted as a part of the Park Place Rangers, you'll have to loosen up. Even then, it's going to be tough for you." Bobby drove toward their assigned district as he spoke.

Within minutes they received a call to check a family disturbance at a home in Sunnyside. When they arrived, they found a husband and wife arguing because the husband had come home late after an evening of drinking. Bobby took the lead in calming the situation and they were cleared from the call in less than 20 minutes.

Not long after returning to service with the dispatcher, they approached an intersection where they saw a car speed through the red light.

"Ready for your first traffic ticket?" Bobby asked, turning on the overhead emergency lights.

James didn't say anything, but he picked up the clipboard with a ticket book attached that lay in the seat between them.

When the car pulled over, they approached the vehicle, with Bobby standing a few feet behind his partner to see how he handled his first ticket. The rookie, though a little nervous, handled the traffic stop by the book. Luckily, the violator, a middle-aged woman, admitted running the red light, apologized, and then signed the ticket without any argument.

As they returned to the car, Bobby commented, "Good work."

At midnight Bobby acknowledged a call regarding a fight in progress at The Blues Bar on Reed Road. They arrived on the scene in less than five minutes. As they entered the bar they saw several customers standing at the edge of a small dance floor watching a man and woman screaming at each other. Blood dripped onto the collar of the man's shirt from a scratch on his neck.

"What's going on?" Bobby asked, stepping onto the dance floor between the two combatants who had stopped screaming.

“Bitch tried to cut me,” the man complained. “She got a knife!”

Bobby stepped toward the woman who moved her right hand behind her leg. “Let me see your hands,” Bobby ordered, reaching for her right arm.

The woman turned, raising the knife as if to swing it toward him. Bobby reacted instinctively; striking the woman’s left cheek with the back of his hand. She stumbled backward as the knife flew through the air before hitting the floor and sliding to a stop just under a juke box against the back wall.

Turning, Bobby saw that other patrons of the bar were surging toward him.

One of them threatened, “Po-lice don’t need to be hittin’ our women!”

The crowd’s movement stopped suddenly, at the sound of a revolver being cocked.

“Which one of you muthafucka’s want some of this?” James screamed, while pointing his pistol at the crowd.

Everyone backed away from the edge of the dance floor. Bobby slapped handcuffs on the woman, recovered the knife from the floor, and told his partner to follow him to the car. Outside, Bobby placed the woman in the patrol car.

Most of the customers had stayed inside, but the man who had been arguing with the woman followed them out to ask what they were going to do with her.

Figuring the man already had remorse about the incident, Bobby responded as he opened the car door, "We'll just file a simple assault charge on her. You can bail her out in an hour or so."

After completing the paperwork and booking their prisoner at the central jail, Bobby drove back to their district. While driving, he explained to James why the woman had been arrested.

"If you have to put your hands on someone, they've got to go to jail. Always remember that and it will save you a lot of grief. It's hard to justify physical contact with someone who doesn't belong in jail. Appreciate what you did back there at the bar." Bobby continued. "Just remember; don't ever pull it unless you're willing to use it."

When they gathered for roll-call the next night, everyone had heard the story. Bobby's new rookie was going to be alright, no matter what his color.

*****

Five years later it was not unusual for a white and black cop to ask the sergeant if they might be assigned to ride as regular partners. James Young, however, never became a part of one of those salt-and-pepper teams. When asked by a young officer years later, why, if he was the first to ride with a white guy, that he didn't ever have a white partner, he replied, "My daddy used to say, 'the one who plows the field doesn't necessarily have to stay for the harvest.' I guess I had my share of riding with white cops when I was a rookie."

BABY, IT WAS A SAD FEELING!

She sat in the back seat of the patrol car crying. Mascara ran down her cheeks. Her blouse had been torn and she held it together with one hand. Nelson Ralston and Larry Lassiter were attempting to get a description of the rapist who had abducted her while she waited at a red light in Houston's ship channel area. They had just asked her for a description of the man.

"He was black, in his early 20's. He was wearing a tuxedo! I remember seeing the little iridescent blue button studs down the front of his shirt that matched the cufflinks."

The two officers looked at each other for a moment. This was the fourth rape in the area in the last three months. Two of the previous victims had been abducted similarly to the victim they had in the car. The third had a flat tire and had gotten out of her car when she was attacked. All described a young black man wearing a tuxedo as the suspect. None of the victims were residents of the area, but were passing through late at night, either on the way home from an evening-shift job or from a night out with friends.

When the ambulance arrived to take the victim to the county hospital, the officers helped her from their car. The ambulance attendants insisted that she get on the stretcher they unloaded from the ambulance. Soon the officers stood alone beside her car. It would be towed downtown and gone over closely for evidence.

As they waited for a wrecker, Nelson kicked the rear tire of the car in frustration.

"You know its Willie Nash that is doing this! Maybe this one can identify him, but I doubt it. None of the others have."

Willie Nash was a young black man who lived in the project. He had been arrested once by the two officers as he climbed out the window of a low-rent motel, The Pyramid Courts, just down the street from where they waited. Willie Nash received a probated sentence for the burglary.

There were more than 20 unsolved burglary cases at the motel. In every case, the suspect had entered through an open window in one of the un-air-conditioned rooms. He would then look for the motel occupant's trousers where he would often find a wallet.

Several of the victims had awakened while he was still in the room and described him as a young, tall, black man. In every instance he had escaped through the window. Only once had the victim attempted to stop him. That victim had been rewarded with a broken nose and two chipped teeth.

Nelson and Larry were convinced that Willie was responsible for all the rapes and burglaries. They had stopped him one night as he walked out of the apartment project where he lived with his mother. He had been wearing a tuxedo. The officers spoke with the assistant district attorney about him, but there was not enough evidence to charge him without a victim who could identify him as the rapist.

*****

Three weeks later, just a little after midnight on a Sunday, the dispatcher called their radio number.

"Make the shooting at the Pyramid Courts, room number seventeen. Ambulance is in route."

Nelson and Larry sped to the Pyramid Courts, a motel that had several permanent guests who rented by the month. When they got to room seventeen, they were met by a woman they both knew. Jackie was the night bartender at Seven Seas Lounge. It was a bar only a few blocks from the Pyramid Courts, where sailors and stevedores met to drink and fight.

Jackie, who was about 50 years old, showed all the wear and tear of a career barmaid. She had been an attractive woman at an earlier time in her life, but 25 years of smoke-filled barrooms and nasty-tempered boyfriends had taken their toll.

She was a good referee for the nearly nightly fights at the Seven Seas, but at least once every weekend she had to call for the help of a uniform. It was usually Nelson and Larry who answered the call.

"What happened, Jackie?" Larry began.

"I killed the son-of-a-bitch. He's layin' in there beside my bed," she said in a voice coarsened by years of cigarette smoke and whiskey. As she spoke, she moved to the side and pointed further into the room.

The two officers walked the few steps to the bedroom. Like most motel rooms, there was a bed, a night stand, and room for little else. Willie Nash was slumped in a seated position on the floor between the wall and the bed, leaning against the night stand. Five small bullet holes marked his forehead, just above the eyebrows. He was wearing a tuxedo and his shirt had iridescent blue studs and cufflinks. He stared straight at Nelson with an expression in death as if he was confused about what had happened. A small revolver lay on the bed beside him.

"You know him, Jackie?" Larry asked.

"I know him. It's Willie Nash. He hangs around the Courts here all the time looking for something to steal."

"What's he doing in your bedroom?" Nelson asked.

"I walked home when I closed the bar. I came in and went straight to the bedroom, ready for a night's sleep. When I turned on the lamp beside the bed, he grabbed me. I don't know how he got in, but he nearly twisted my neck half off my head. I fell over on the night stand. I guess he hadn't seen my pistol. I leave it there under a Readers Digest.

"I grabbed it as I fell. He took a hand full of my hair and pulled me up, then pushed me onto the bed. When he bent over me, I slid out and stood up with him between me and the nightstand.

"I pointed the gun at his head and pulled the trigger. Baby, let me tell you! That was a sad feeling when it just went click! But I just kept pulling the trigger. Next five times all worked fine. Sixth time it went click again, but Willie was on the floor by then."

For the next two hours, the officers worked the crime scene with Homicide detectives and the investigators who took photos and gathered evidence. They then transported Jackie to the Homicide office where she would make and sign a statement regarding the night's events. They left her there and on the way to their patrol car, stopped by the photography lab.

"Hey, guys. When you get the photos processed from the shooting at the Pyramid Courts, will you send us a blown-up copy of the dead guy?" Nelson asked.

"No problem," the clerk replied. "You guys get this close to all your victims? Wanting photos and all?"

"Nope, Willie Nash is just a special case," Nelson replied as they walked out.

*****

Two years after the shooting call to the Pyramid Courts, Nelson Ralston was in the locker room at Houston's Park Place police substation. He was cleaning out his locker in preparation for his new assignment in the Helicopter Division. He would begin as an observer and later become a helicopter pilot for the Houston P.D. Eddie Jackson walked in as Nelson began packing.

"Who's the dead guy?" Eddie asked, looking over Nelson's shoulder at the crime scene photo of Willie Nash, taped to the locker door.

"He was just a young East End turd who didn't quite make it." Nelson responded, continuing to remove things from his locker. "But he never got caught on anything but a burglary one time, even though he raped and ruined the lives of several good women who just happened to be in the wrong place."

"Who got him? Did you shoot him?" Eddie was curious now.

"Nope. He was shot by a woman who told me and Lassiter what a 'sad feeling it is to point a pistol at a rapist, and hear a click when you pull the trigger.' Luckily the next five times sent .22 slugs right into his sorry face."

Nelson shut the door and picked up the box with his belongings. "You can have the photo if you want it. I always liked to look at it to remind me that justice doesn't always come with a pair of handcuffs or a conviction in court. Sometimes, the right thing just happens."

Larry Watts

BLUE THOUGHTS ON SNIFFIN' AND CRUISIN'

Bernie Stratham had been a sergeant at Houston's Park Place police substation for nearly a year and by most standards, he was a lucky guy. He'd spent seven years as a night-shift officer at Park Place. It was one of the best patrol jobs in the city: lots of action, a good work group, and plenty of off-duty jobs available if he needed extra cash.

When he was promoted to sergeant, Bernie spent only six months at the downtown station before an opening at Park Place allowed him to come back home. He worked days, which was nearly unheard of for a newly-promoted sergeant. But others had not wanted the day job. It fit well with Bernie's desire to work with his son's little league team.

It was Sunday morning and he had just left the coffee shop on Telephone Road when the disturbance call was broadcast by the dispatcher. Park Place was operating short-staffed, so Bernie volunteered to check the disturbance. The neighborhood was a middle-class subdivision that generated few calls for police service.

When he stopped at the address, Bernie was met by a man who appeared to be about 60 years old.

"It's my son, officer. Jack's on drugs again. He climbed a tree in the backyard and won't come down. He's been up there howling like a wolf for an hour. It's embarrassing. We've lived in this neighborhood for thirty years."

"Just you and your son live here, Mr.... what was that name?" Bernie asked.

"Cecil Johnson. My wife is in the house, embarrassed, and quite frankly, too afraid of our son to come out." Mr. Johnson stared at the ground.

The two men walked through the home and out the back door. Mrs. Johnson did not appear. When he stepped onto the patio just outside the door, Bernie heard a shrieking similar to the sound monkeys sometimes make. He looked up into a single oak tree. Staring back at him was a long-haired young man in a t-shirt and cut-off jeans. He was barefoot and soaking wet. It was February and 50 degrees this morning. The man was shivering.

"What's going on up there?" Bernie asked.

"Just being alive, officer. But I ain't comin' down. You can't make me." As he said this, he scooted further up the branch he was sitting on.

"How'd you get wet?" Bernie asked, ignoring the challenge.

"He did it. He thinks he can make me come down. But I won't." The man nodded toward his father and began howling and looking to the sky.

"Sir, would you go back inside while I talk to him. What's his name again?" Bernie asked.

"He's Cecil James, Jr., but we've always called him Jack," the father said as he turned and entered the house.

Bernie looked around the patio and saw a metal lawn chair. He pulled it to a spot where he could sit and see Jack without straining his neck.

After he was seated, he asked, "So Jack, what are you on? You been sniffing?"

"Oh yeah, man. I got a whole case of Krylon spray paint in the garage. Clear, no color. You can't even see it around my nose, can you?"

"No, no evidence. If you're going to sniff, always get the clear paint. How long you plan to stay up there?"

"Doesn't make any difference. I'll come down when I decide," Jack replied.

"Oh, I got that message. I just need to know because if the neighbors start complaining, I'll have to get a fire truck out here and use their ladder to come get you. I'm sure you don't want that, and me, I'm afraid of heights. So maybe if I know how long you plan to stay there, I can explain it and save us both a lot of trouble."

"I'm gonna stay here till he quits raggin' on me for sniffing glue. Hey, those stripes on your shoulder, that makes you a sergeant, doesn't it? Why'd they send a sergeant out here?"

"I was close by and volunteered to take the call. I'm glad I did, because I think you and I can figure this out. If you don't want your dad complaining about your glue sniffing, why don't you come down and we'll leave here. Go to the Park Place station, dry you off and maybe get a cup of coffee to warm you up." Bernie knew the invitation to warm up would appeal to Jack.

After 15 minutes of continued conversation, Jack finally decided to come down after Bernie promised not to handcuff him. As soon as he was on the ground, Bernie guided him through the backyard to the patrol car. He had been worried that Jack would want to go through the house, which might have created an entirely new set of problems.

Bernie knew he was taking a chance, letting Jack sit up front without handcuffs, but the gamble worked. By the time they arrived at the substation, they were best of friends, at least for the moment. Bernie gave Jack a towel and a cup of coffee, which he drank sitting in the sergeant's office.

He then suggested that Jack lay down for a while. He led him to one of the temporary holding cells without a problem. Jack was now in jail for public intoxication and Bernie was sure that his parents would be around in a few hours to post their son's bond. It was a sad, dysfunctional relationship, but at least no one was hurt this time.

Back in his car, Bernie checked the time. It was nearly noon. He decided to drive by the delicatessen about a mile from the substation and get a hoagie sandwich for lunch. He'd bring it back to the station to eat.

When he approached the intersection a half-block from the eatery, his was the third vehicle from the red light. A motorcycle was stopped waiting for the light to turn green and the car between them was not quite to the intersection. It was a yellow Chrysler, driven by a silver-haired woman. As she approached the motorcycle, it appeared that she wasn't paying attention. She hit the rear wheel of the bike with just enough momentum to knock the rider to the ground.

The next seconds were frenzied. The woman reversed her car and backed up slightly as Bernie exited his car behind her. The cyclist stood, but the cuff of his jeans was caught in the motorcycle chain. Almost immediately, the cycle burst into flame from gasoline spilled on the hot exhaust. When she saw this, the driver of the Chrysler pulled around the flaming cycle and sped away.

Bernie ran toward the man who was attempting to disentangle himself from the motorcycle, but in seconds the man's body was engulfed in flames. He struggled for what seemed like only a second or two, as Bernie ran toward him pulling his jacket off. An attempt to try to smother the flames was too late. The body, crisp brown, with skin broken and clothes burned off, lay in a near fetal position beside the cycle. The flames disappeared as quickly as they had erupted.

A few minutes later the yellow Chrysler pulled to a stop across the street. An elderly man got out and walked toward Bernie. An ambulance, a fire truck and two police cars were a half-block away with red lights flashing and sirens blaring.

"Officer, my wife was involved in this accident. She panicked when she saw the fire. Is the guy on the motorcycle alright?"

*****

That afternoon, Bernie learned that the dead cyclist was a 23-year-old father returning home from work when he was killed. The irony of the two incidents with two young men was not lost on him. What kind of justice allows one young man to torment his parents and destroy his life, while another, who apparently took responsibility seriously, is killed in a freak accident? There was no little league practice that afternoon, but Bernie would hold his son close when he arrived home at the end of his shift.

THE SPEEDER

It was Christmas Eve and Nelson Ralston wished he was home with his kids instead of patrolling the streets of southeast Houston. His only consolation was that when he got off at six on Christmas morning, he could spend a couple of hours with the two of them as they opened their presents.

He was on his way to a prowler call when the dispatcher advised him that the call had been canceled. As he had been driving down Telephone Road from the Park Place station, he'd noticed a car following him not more than two car-lengths behind and at the same rate of speed, about 45 miles per hour, as he had been enroute to the call. He slowed down to 35 when the call was canceled and the car behind began flashing his high-beam lights. Nelson turned on his emergency lights, pulled to the side of the road and met the driver of the other car at the rear of the patrol car.

"You were speeding," the man said. "I followed you for nearly a mile and you were driving 45 in a 35 zone. You deserve a ticket! I want you to call another officer to meet us to write you up."

Nelson first thought it was a joke. He smiled at the guy and waited for the punch line.

"I don't know why you're smiling," the man continued. "You have no more right to break the law than anyone else. Are you going to call someone over to write the ticket?"

"Let me see your driver's license," Nelson responded.

"No, this isn't about me! It's about you obeying the law!" The man was quickly becoming agitated.

"Mr., let me tell you, before this gets out of hand, give me your driver's license or I will have to place you under arrest."

The man reluctantly complied and Nelson walked back to his car and got his ticket book.

"Now let me explain something to you," Nelson began. "You have no authority to stop anyone and make accusations that they broke traffic laws, especially a police officer. It just happens that I was on my way to a prowler call when you were following me. But you're going to get yourself in a real bind, doing what you just did."

The man interrupted, "Don't start that stuff. You don't accept excuses from the drivers you write tickets to and I won't either."

Nelson made up his mind at that moment. "How fast did you say we were going? Was it 45?" He asked as he began writing a ticket for speeding.

When he had finished, he advised the man that he must sign the ticket and that he could go to court. Although he was furious, the man signed and took his copy of the ticket, ranting as he walked back to his car that this was not over.

Shortly thereafter, Nelson was on his way and the other car made a U-turn and headed back in the direction of the Park Place substation. Later that night, Nelson was called to the station because the speeder had shown up there and made a complaint. He wrote a letter of explanation and the matter was resolved.

*****

One year later, again on Christmas Eve, Nelson Ralston and Larry Lassiter turned onto Telephone Road just after leaving the Park Place police substation. The two had been riding as partners for about nine months. If he had to work on Christmas Eve, Nelson was glad that he at least had some company this year.

Less than a block after they turned onto Telephone Road, a car approached from the other direction. One of its headlights was not working. Larry turned the patrol car around and soon they had the other car stopped. When Nelson approached the driver's window he saw that it was the same man with whom he'd had the encounter the previous Christmas Eve. However, there was no sign that the driver recognized Nelson.

"Sir, we stopped you because one of your headlights is out. Can I see your driver's license please?" Nelson asked.

The man handed him the license and Nelson asked him if he had been aware that the light was out. The man said he had not known.

"Excuse me, I'll be right back," Nelson said. He then went back to the patrol car and called in a warrant check on the man's name. The report soon came back that there was a warrant because the man had not paid the speeding ticket from the previous year.

That's amazing," Larry said. "I guess we'll ruin his Christmas again this year."

"I don't think so," Nelson replied. "Did you see those toys in the back seat? There's a kid or maybe more than one at home expecting to get those toys. Let's be a little innovative."

Nelson walked back to the driver's window, handed the man his license and told him to get the headlight fixed. When Nelson told him he was free to go, the look of surprise on the man's face convinced Nelson that he remembered.

Two nights later, when they left the station, Larry and Nelson drove to the man's house. When he came to the door, they arrested him for the speeding warrant. The errant driver had been correct last year when he told Nelson that the matter wasn't over, but it would be, when he paid his fine and got out of jail.

Larry Watts

The Shoeshine Man

Larry Lassiter got off work at 5:30 Saturday morning. He was a sergeant at Houston's Park Place police substation, where he'd previously worked as a patrolman. Divorced for nearly a year, he lived in an apartment not far from the station. He drove home, went to his apartment and fell into bed. Having worked an extra job all day on Friday, he fell asleep in minutes. His much-needed rest lasted only an hour and fifteen minutes before his phone rang.

"Lassiter," he answered in a hoarse, weary voice.

"Sorry to interrupt your nap," Sergeant Henderson said, "but your night-shift desk officer fucked up big time last night."

Henderson was the day-shift sergeant who had relieved him, and Larry knew that he wasn't sorry to have called at all. Henderson enjoyed pointing out the mistakes of others.

"Your guys booked two drunks last night, one white and the other black. Richard Soward, the white guy, came in at midnight and the other guy, Herman Wright, came in about two hours later. The first one had about $700 cash that was inventoried and the second guy had zip.

"When your desk officer, I think it was Jones, went back to get the white guy to let him post bond, he was asleep and didn't answer, but Wright answered for him.

"Jones bonded Wright out with Soward's money and gave him all of Soward's personal items, including credit cards."

Larry was wide awake now. "So did you just discover this?"

"Yeah, we went back to get Wright to transfer him to the downtown jail and realized that there had been a screw up. We also found the wallet with Soward's driver's license and other identification in the bushes beside the front door, but no cash or credit cards.

"We've released Soward, but somebody's got to give him his money back. That somebody probably should also hope like hell that there are no charges on the cards."

Larry was sitting on the side of his bed now, absorbing the information.

"What address did Wright give when he was booked?" he asked.

Larry could hear the other sergeant shuffling papers just before he replied, "In the projects off La Porte Road and Broadway."

"I'll be there in a few minutes," Larry replied.

He hung up; reached for a small phone book from his uniform shirt pocket and found the number he wanted.

Howard Stassen, a black man, shined shoes at the airport. He also owned a nightclub which was located next door to his home, on La Porte Road, just a few blocks from the housing project Sergeant Henderson had referred to.

Larry had known Howard since he worked at Park Place before being promoted to sergeant. Larry and his partner had dropped by the club sporadically to visit with him. Although there was an occasional fight and sometimes customers would start a dice game on the side of the building, Howard ran a pretty respectable business. The partners could count on him to let them know about serious crime in the neighborhood, such as the information he provided regarding a rapist who had terrorized the area a few years earlier.

It was nearly eight o'clock on Saturday morning and the phone rang only once.

"Stassen," a deep but friendly voice answered.

"Howard, Larry Lassiter. How you doing, man?" Larry asked.

"Good Sarge. What's going on to cause you to call this time of day? You ought to be asleep."

Larry explained what happened, told Howard the guy's name and where he lived.

"Let me do some checking. I don't recognize the name, but I can find out. You at the station?" Howard asked.

"No, but I will be in fifteen minutes. Call me there if you get anything."

Larry hung up the phone, put his uniform on, and drove back to the station. When he arrived, Sergeant Henderson and his desk officer, Carl Matlock, were waiting for him.

"Damn, Lassiter. You night-shift guys can't tell a black drunk from a white one?" Henderson grinned and winked at Matlock.

Before he could answer, the phone rang. Matlock answered and handed the receiver to Larry.

"Hey, Sarge. It's Howard. Your guy is a block down the street from my place at that little convenience store. He's around on the side sitting against the building drinking wine. But you better get down here pretty soon. The guy at the store said he already bought three bottles of that Boones Farm Strawberry Hill."

"I'm on the way. Thanks, Howard. You're a good friend."

Larry told Henderson what he had learned and, to his surprise, the sergeant offered to ride with him to make the arrest.

In less than 10 minutes the two sergeants had handcuffed Herman Wright, searched him, and placed him in the back seat of the car. They recovered $587.21 from him, leaving only $17.47 of the other prisoner's money unaccounted for.

The credit cards were in his pocket. Wright said they had not been used. He was taken back to the substation before being transported downtown and charged with theft.

The night-shift desk officer, Percy Jones, was waiting when the sergeants arrived. He was apologetic and embarrassed. Sergeant Henderson suggested he should be suspended for the mistake, but Lassiter quickly advised the other sergeant that it was a night-shift matter and none of his concern.

When Richard Soward was contacted, he returned to the station, where he was given the money and credit cards. Officer Jones kicked in his own money to make up the $17.47 loss. He received a reprimand for the mistake.

A week later officers on the evening-shift raided Howard Stassen's night club and found that one of his customers was intoxicated. They arrested the customer and Howard. He was charged with serving an intoxicated person an alcoholic drink. The fine was $200 and the license for the nightclub was suspended for 30 days.

Howard never complained. He knew he lived and ran a business in a crime-ridden neighborhood. The police were not his enemy even though at times he was the target of arrests related to his bar business. The relationship was personal with some of the officers, ten of whom he had home phone numbers for. Each year on Christmas morning he called each of them with holiday greetings. At a time when racial tension was high, Howard and those officers bridged the racial divide.

INTERNAL AFFAIRS

He heard the heels of her shoes tapping against the tile floor in the airport terminal. Larry Lassiter knew it was the woman he had come to the airport to meet. He stopped, turned, and waited for her.

His friend, Howard Stassen, ran a shoeshine stand at the airport and knew that Larry had recently divorced. Believing that he wasn't dealing with it well, Howard had decided to intercede. He arranged for Larry to meet Rebecca Long at the airport for coffee.

Rebecca worked as a security officer monitoring passengers checking in for flights. When there were no flights to monitor, she hung out at the shoeshine stand, as several airport employees did. They liked talking with Howard, who was friendly and a well-known character at the airport. When Howard learned that she too was recently divorced, he thought she and Larry might make a good match.

Although Larry realized his friend wanted to help, he wasn't thrilled about the blind date. He had arrived at the airport just before the agreed upon time, but Rebecca wasn't there. He bid Howard good-bye and headed for the exit. And that's when he had heard the click of her heels.

After Rebecca introduced herself and apologized for being late, they agreed to a cup of coffee at the airport diner. The conversation was friendly, but there was no spark between them. After a few pleasantries and details from each regarding their current status, they shook hands and departed. Rebecca returned to her work duties. Larry left the airport.

He knew he would never use the phone number she had written on a napkin. Larry thought she seemed too eager as he tossed the napkin in the trash on the way out. He had fulfilled his obligation to Howard by meeting the woman. If only his friends would stop trying to engineer his new life.

Two years later, Larry sat in the sergeants' office at the Park Place police substation visiting with his old friend, Doc Smithers. Doc had been the desk officer before being assigned to the newly created Internal Affairs Division. After completing that assignment, he had happily returned a week before. The two were catching up on their lives since Doc had been away. There was a pause in the conversation as both sipped coffee and relaxed.

"You know, Sarge, I was really worried about that deal at the airport. I held my breath hoping you wouldn't say anything that might be misconstrued," Doc said.

The inquisitive expression on Larry's face told Doc he had begun a conversation he would have been wise to avoid.

"What are you talking about, the 'deal at the airport'?" Larry asked.

"Sarge, are you saying you didn't know about the investigation of you and that black shoeshine man at the airport?"

"Not a clue. No one has ever said anything to me about any investigation." A hint of anger caused his cheeks to blush. "So tell me about it."

"Well, I probably shouldn't, but I guess I've already opened it up. There was a sergeant who worked for the Airport Police Department and he knew that female security guard you met at the diner. His name was Reed, I think. At I.A. we all thought he was probably screwing her or at least trying to.

"He called and said there was a Park Place sergeant who was running whores with the shoeshine man at the airport. When Reed heard from the girl that the black guy was setting up a meeting between the two of you, he was sure that you were meeting her to try to convince her to start turning tricks for your prostitution business."

Larry interrupted, "You're telling me that there was an investigation of my personal life based on some asshole's theory that I was a pimp? Unbelievable!"

"That day at the airport when you met her, she was wearing a wire," Doc continued. "She chased you down because you got there a few minutes early and they were still putting the wire on. Once you met and didn't talk about anything but your kids, how you didn't like blind dates, and that you didn't think you were ready to start dating, we all breathed a sigh of relief.

"That is, everyone from I.A. was relieved. Sergeant Reed was still convinced he had discovered a major prostitution ring. But when you didn't call her back, we closed the file about six months later. I just assumed that someone had told you about it."

Larry sat in stunned silence. The Internal Affairs Division was still fairly new in H.P.D., but if this was an indication of their work, things were changing, and not for the better.

He went home that night and thought about his career. He'd spent two years in the Vice Squad before being promoted to sergeant. He remembered having arrested a call girl on a sting and finding her "trick book" when he processed her into the jail. He had discreetly taken the spiral notebook and copied the pages before returning it to her property.

When he and his partner had reviewed the entries in the book, they found the name of a local television news reporter with his phone number in the list of "johns" or "tricks." In another section of the notes were the names of several women, some of whom the two partners recognized as high dollar call girls. Among these names was one that shocked them both. It was that of a highly respected police woman who worked in the Juvenile Division.

They had discussed their findings with a veteran Vice Division sergeant. Should they set up a sting on the police woman, using the newsman's name as a reference? Larry would never forget what the sergeant had said.

"Guys, I will never tell you not to pursue any investigation. I will tell you something I've learned working in Vice for a lot of years.

"For the most part, people don't want us to enforce vice laws. Lots of people either like to gamble, drink after hours, or chase prostitutes. Hell, just during my time up here, we've had one mayor caught up in a gambling sting and another who chased the street whores in the early morning hours.

"What's important about our work is that we get to know lots of street people who are the underbelly of Houston society. When a big case goes down, like a contract killing or a big robbery, and the detectives can't seem to get a lead, those connections with the dregs of society can be worth more than all the vice arrests made last year. We've helped solve some pretty important crimes just by having the trust of some of those people.

"My suggestion is that you use the name of the newsman john to work some of the other whores, but why go after another officer? Don't forget, we all have to work extra jobs. Do you think she's doing anything worse than officers working off-duty security at a nightclub when they know the only reason the owner hires them is to keep other officers from coming in and harassing his customers?"

At the time, the sergeant's words made sense. Larry and his partner never used the information about the police woman. But, with the advent of Internal Affairs, he knew that a new day was evolving at the Houston Police Department.

ABOUT THE AUTHOR

Larry Watts worked as a police officer for 21 years. He left that career to represent police officers across Texas in employment matters, including officer involved shootings. He now writes novels and enjoys life on the Gulf Coast with his wife, Carolyn.

A message from Larry:

If you enjoyed these stories, please let me know. I can be contacted at Larry@LarryWatts.net. You can also visit my website at www.LarryWatts.net, and connect with me on Facebook and Twitter.

Other books by Larry Watts

Right, Wrong, & Rationalizing Truth (2011)

Cheating Justice (2012)

Beautiful Revenge (a short story 2012)

Made in the USA
San Bernardino, CA
08 February 2017